Red Roses & Rosemary

Elsie Shears

Red Roses
&
Rosemary

Elsie Shears

Volume II

310 Kennington Road SE11 4LD

Issued by Volume II*
Printed and bound by BWD Ltd., Northolt, Middx.
ISBN 1 85846 020 4

*An imprint of The Professional Authors' & Publishers Association

Chapter One

This is the story of a girl born in the East End of London in 1907. Her father was a stevedore in the East London Docks; her mother, like most other women of her station in life, was hard-worked, poor, harassed and consequently short-tempered. The neighbours in Gold Street, Stepney, were mostly Jews who had gradually filtered into London and spread themselves around Bethnal Green, Whitechapel and Commercial Road.

Emma Greaves' childhood seemed to be filled with memories of the kitchen filled with steam as her mother washed clothes, usually for the Jewish neighbours; of Friday evenings, with her mother keeping their fires alight; of ironing, and the secret forbidden meals eaten in the kitchen during the passover; the mysterious women who came and went from the front room upstairs. She still had the memory of her mother washing for the notorious 'Peter the Painter' before the Sydney Street affair. Monday morning was given over to 'Uncle's', where Father's best suit was elevated on a hanger in a mysterious region above the pawnshop counter in order not to get creased.

Friday was the day when mother retrieved it ready for Father's usual week-end jaunts to the local, the Coopers Arms.
She, poor woman, would be very secretive about the whole affair, but as Emma got older she was confident that the twinkle she saw in her Father's eye as he brushed himself down ready to join his pals was his way of saying: 'You have nothing on me, Mother. I know where this has been all week'. Rushing home after the business transactions with 'Uncle', Mother would add the cash she had received to make up the rent for the landlord. It would lie very correctly on the parlour table on top of the rent book, and at precisely 2 p.m, in answer to a rat-a-tat-tat, the door would be opened to Mr Jesperson who would enter the passage, remove his top hat and enter the parlour. He would place his Gladstone bag on the floor beside the chair he occupied, take out his spectacles, adjust them on the tip of his nose and count the money, saying as he popped it into his bag, 'Quite correct, quite correct'. He would sign the book 'clear' and

then look at Emma. The remarks were always the same: "Nice child, nice child. Come and take your weekly penny and say, Thank you, Mr. Jesperson". Dutifully Emma would respond, and close her hand over the coin. He would depart, the penny would change hands and in return her mother would give a farthing for sweets. Emma was very sorry when she went to school, for it was then that this little ritual ended.

School days began at Dempsey Street Council School. Most of the children were Jewish, and therefore the many holidays of their religion had to be observed. Emma's mother often said she was fed up with it, For she had sent Emma to school to get her out of the way, not to see her run the bloody streets. So Emma was taken to Red Coat, a Church School. She was unhappy there; she disliked prayers and religious instruction. It was sufficient to be sent to Sunday School in order to be taken out in a brake to Epping Forest, and to go to a Christmas party. Emma decided she would alter all this one day. In the meantime she had to do as she was told. It was better than the buckle end of her mother's belt that came very frequently into action when she misbehaved.

As she grew older her life became harder. Her father suddenly died of a cerebral haemorrhage. She did not miss him very much. He had been kind when ever they met, but he had had his own drinking pals, and sometimes Mum would 'pop up the top' to join them.

Somewhere in the background of the family adult life was a hazy brother who was married and lived in Clerkenwell, and then there was a sister, Ruth, who had left home, lived in Canning Town, and had since been married. Emma liked to weave mystery round the family, they were all so old to her, gradually the mysterious thoughts were voiced and, within her special gang, sworn to secrecy. She told them that she came from another family who was rich, but had asked this family to care for her until they returned from America.

"Where's America?" said her special friend Willy Martain.

"Cor! can't you tell 'em?" joined in Alfie Hill, who was runner-up to Willy Martain.

"It's a long way from here," replied Emma with a very knowing and confident nod, remembering Bernerd Shapiro who had been in her mother's care for three months whilst his parents actually had gone to America. Emma had hated Bernard while he was with them - he was a boy after all, and her mother always showed a preferance for boys. He used to wet his bed, and would wake up crying - and her mother would say "Never mind", and take him into her own bed, a coveted place for Emma. But if Emma ever wet her pants, my word, her mother would slash her arse, and never take into consideration that she was always <u>clean</u> in bed.

At nine years of age Emma showed signs of a very sharp intellect; she was extremely bright at school, and popular with her teachers. There was a keeness about her and a great thirst for learning. Poverty was an ever-present spectre, and during school days she was given free meals. The hunger within her was so often swamped by feeling of pride that arose when she was given her meal tickets, but eventually she became submissive and accepted what was inevitable. More than ever her mother spent hours at the wash tub, cleaning the houses of neighbouring Jews who showed many kindnesses towards the family. If the poor could not fend for themselves, here remained only the workhouse for the adults and homes for the children.

Mrs Greaves worked hard. Her two adult children never came near her since their father died, and Emma was all she had. By nature she had a hasty temper. Circumstances often forced her to lose control. Frequently her pent-up feelings were given vent over the luckless Emma. Gradually the comforts of the home disappeared, sold sometimes for a few shillings or else pawned in the false hope that when better days came along they could be retrieved. It was a very hopeless state of affairs. On Saturday nights around eleven o'clock, Emma and her mother would go hand in hand to the market in the Old Road. Most of the stalls would be closing down, so that was the time to buy a piece of meat , usually a flank of beef for a shilling; one or two other items would be purchased while Emma crawled under the stalls to salvage anything that looked edible. Into a large black bag would go whatever else she could pick up from the edge of the stall as she crept up.

"Now then, now then!" a stallholder would shout as he saw her, "watcha doing, you little bitch? Get out of `ere!" and Emma would scuttle away. If most of the contents of the bag were stolen, Emma would join her mother as quickly as possible, giving her hand a tug which was a signal to hurry away. They were by then relieved to leave behind the missing lamps, and the last calls of the venders. "Buy, buy, buy - going cheap - come on, missus, try this for the `ole man's breakfast ... "And so back to the little house to look over their spoils. Mrs Greaves had also been busy while Emma scrounged under the stalls, and it was surprising how often there appeared new socks for Emma or a new pinny. No questions were ever asked, no explanations ever given - just "Here you are Em, try this on for size", or "What do you think of my new scarf?"

The kitchen and the front room were the only rooms in the house kept for the family. The others were let out. Two middle-aged men lived separately in the two upstairs back rooms - Emma called them Uncle Reg and Uncle George respectively. In the large room lived a coloured woman from Jamaica - Emma was terrified of her dark skin and scuttled into the kitchen every time she heard her foot-fall. She much preferred the two women who had lived there when Father was alive - They were happy, laughing women, ready to pull her long black hair playfully, and every Saturday night, when they should have been thinking of going to bed, they would be going out, but never forgot to leave a bag of sweets for Sunday morning.

One day Leah, the dark one, suddenly disappeared. Emma was very mystified, and hung around the passage listening to Mother and Rebecca; the words "rot" and "smothered" lingered very long in her memory. Shortly after Leah went, Rebecca married a policeman and went to live in the next road. Mother had once said to Father that policemen often did marry "them there sort". Mr Jesperson had also died, and now Mother had to go to work in an office to pay the rent - she was often a week behind and it was very upsetting when she received a cautionary note. There was no more Sunday School because that was the day Emma stayed in bed, reading her halfpenny comic, playing with her old wooden doll while Mother washed her clothes for Monday. Emma liked that day in bed! Uncle George would sometimes pop in and give her some lemonade, or a bit of fruit - he was very fond of her and always called her Babe. Emma liked that too. She liked it now that she and Mother were alone. Mother confided in her, Mother let her sleep in the big bed with her - they cuddled up together, and Emma was thrilled that Mother let her snooze into one of her ample breasts. She had always wanted to do that when Father was here, but somehow Mother was farther away then. Poor they still were, but everything seemed much more cosy now.

The First World war broke out at a time when living conditions were at their harshest. This was a turning point for them. Mrs Greaves got some temporary work, sitting up at nights with sick old people in a home; nurses were in great demand for military hospitals. Emma was left alone all night for six nights a week. She would lie in bed shivering, frightened to close her eyes, seeing all around the room the dark, red-rimmed eyes of the Jamaican woman. One night she could stand it no longer. Jumping out of bed she rushed upstairs into Uncle George's room. He was asleep, but Emma touched his shoulder and he immediately shot up in bed.

"Uncle George," she said, "I'm frightened!" Her teeth chattered and tears were streaming down her face.

"Eh, what!" said Uncle George sleepily, and then realising what the child had said, he put out a hand and comfortingly chided her.

"There's nothing to fear, Emmy." He got out of bed and lit the table lamp. "Go back to bed." But Emma, now safe in the haven of his room, refused to move.

"Let me stay here, Uncle George - <u>please</u>!"

"No, Babe, you can't stay here." And bending down, he put on his socks to take her back to her bed. In a second, Emma was in bed and had snuggled down into the warm feathers. Uncle George was alarmed.

"Come, Babe," he said coaxingly, "your Mother will tan you hard if she finds you've been here."

"Don't tell her, please, Uncle George," she said with a sob. "I'm so frightened to be alone. Please, please let me stay."

The middle-aged man looked down at the child - he was very fond of her and was disturbed by her tears. His room was small and the only furniture other than the bed, were a chest of drawers, a table and an upright chair.

"All right," he said rather hastily. "Go to sleep." And almost before the words were uttered Emma had drifted away. He stood there, poor man, uncertain as to what he should do. If he went into Reggie's room it would cause a disturbance. He could not sleep in an upright chair, and he had nothing spare to make a bed on the floor. If he went down to get some of Mrs Greaves' bedding, he would have to get it back by early morning. If he went down there to sleep, Emma might wake again and cry out What was he to do? Gently he tuned back the bedclothes, removed the bolster, and placed it down the centre of the bed. He blew out the light, kept on his socks, wrapped his night shirt well down his legs and crept onto the edge of the bed. Gingerly he pulled the covers over him.

"Blimey! not one of those bleeders would believe me," he thought referring to his cronies at the market, where he had a second-hand stall in Petticoat Lane. "Poor little Bugger, to be so perishing frightened! But this won't happen again." But Uncle George did not know Emma! Next morning he woke her at 6 o`clock with a cup of tea, saying "Drink this, Babe, and get down before your Mother gets home. We mustn't tell her, cause she thinks you're a brave girl to be left at night."

By the time Mrs Greaves came home at 8 o'clock Emma was back in her own bed and fast asleep. Every evening she would go to bed and try to get to sleep before her mother left. Sometimes she succeeded, but whether she had slept or not, about midnight the terrible fear of being alone would assail her. Eyes would watch her from every corner of the room, and with a dart she would be out of bed, up the stairs and into Uncle George's room like lightning. He had come to accept it; she would dart over the bolster which now occupied a permanent place down the centre of the bed, and immediately go to sleep. Each morning she drank her tea, ran down to her rightful bed, and for six whole months the secret kept.

Then suddenly into the family home came an usurper! At least that was the name Emma would have called the blind woman if she had known it. She was a widow who had lost her sight some years earlier and had been living in the home where Mrs Greaves worked. By some arrangement unknown to Emma, her Mother had been able to change to day work when the authorities of the home had given their consent for Maggie Peters to live out. A small allowance was made for her keep. Emma was told to call her Auntie Maggie. Emma hated it all. Auntie Maggie now slept with Mother. A bed was made up on an old sofa for Emma. Gradually the little talks and intimacies that she enjoyed faded away - the two women got on very well together. Blind Maggie may have been, but Emma always felt she had 'inner eyes'. She always knew what was going on - such as the time Emma went into the food cupboard and began to eat the condensed milk.

"What are you pinching out of the cupboard, my Lady? I'll tell your Mother when she comes home." Or "Stop reading them there books, you know your Mother don't like you reading."

"Oh, shut up, and mind your own business," Emma would shout, "always interfering. My Mum is always hitting me because you tell tales on me. Go back to where you come from."

"All right, my Lady," Maggie would say, "I'll settle for you." She took a fiendish delight in getting Emma strapped.

Time crept on, London was raided, and Emma would stand with the others at night in the passage when the sirens sounded, and listen to the drone of the Zeppelins. Big Bertha, the anti-aircraft gun, was run on a truck up and down the roads in an effort to shell down the enemy, but never succeeded. Lights were dimmed, and the street lamps were blacked out. It was terrifying to go out in the dark. In fact Emma refused to go out after a dreadful experience of being called by a man, who stepped from a doorway as she was coming back from the baker's. At first she stopped, then, terrified, rushed past him as the dim light from a nearby lamp fell across him. She thought his hands were going to grab her, but they were otherwise engaged. Her mother, a fearless woman, went out to find him, but he had drifted into the darkness, satisfied for the moment, no doubt preparing for another victim.

Life was getting very difficult for Emma. There was quite a lot going on inside her. She was now twelve years old. Her breasts were very developed, and consequently her clothes were tight. The boys looked and grinned at each other. Willy was not too bad, and after telling her that her pinny stuck out, and getting his face smacked, he never referred to anything personal again. Saturday night was bath night. A huge bowl of hot water was placed on the kitchen table and her mother washed her down as far as possible, then placing the bowl on the floor, washed up as far as possible. As she grew older Emma was not quite sure of the meaning of the word "possible".

Then, of course, came the inevitable time when her mother said, "You are a woman now," adding quite shrewdly, "You don't tell anyone about this, and keep away from the boys."

Emma had known all about this for ages through her friends - much, of course incorrectly told. Babies, and how they came about, were no secret, but none the less remained a mystery to Emma. When large families lived in confined spaces there could be little hidden, and the whisperings at night could often be heard by the children who shared the marital bed. Emma had none of these experiences, which most of her friends had, but she relished what they had to tell.

Boys of her age were of great interest to Emma. She enjoyed their company, and their games. At first they resented her, but she would hang around them as they played. One day when they were playing rounders with a hard ball and stick, Albert Piggotty, a boy who resented her very much, missed fire and his ball landed clean through a window. Seeing the potential crisis, everyone scuttled off except Albert and the watching Emma. Albert stood petrified and within a few seconds the occupier of the house caught him by the collar and given him a sound whack over the head. It would have been useless to expect money to replace it, as Alberts widowed mother was at home dying from cancer. Emma calmly watched, and when the whacking and threats had ceased, she picked up Alberts cap and stick, gave him the last of a few rather dirty sticky sweets, and followed him as he went to seek his pals. Albert said nothing, but from then on Emma was accepted and joined in all their boyish games. Auntie Maggie would at times ask Emma who she had been playing with, and Emma, thinking it would be of interest, would tell her Aunt all the games she played in the street with the boys. Whether Aunt Maggie had a warped mind, or whether she thought herself responsible for Emma's behaviour while her mother was at work, was never quite clear to Emma, but it was nothing unusual to receive a 'good hiding' from Mother, and afterwards to be told: "That, my Lady, is for playing with the boys," with the added explanation, "Auntie Maggie told me." But nothing ever daunted Emma for long, and next day she would be seen playing leap-frog, or football, or diabolo, or whatever games the boys were playing.

Next to playing with the boys was the interest in reading. Her mother thought it was a waste of time, and set her many jobs to do in the house. These were done quickly in order to get to the latest acquired book. During the time her mother was home these were hidden on the laths under the palliasse of her mattress. Then, of course, by some unknown and remarkable instinct, Auntie Maggie discovered this secret reading. Emma had taken <u>Uncle Tom's Cabin</u> into the lavatory to read, a place which she found was often vacant. Auntie Maggie called her to remove a kettle from the hob, and in her haste she had left the book behind.

"Oh, so that's your game!" she said when she came upon the unretrieved book. "You're a cunning little bitch. Your mother don't know the half of what you get up to."

Emma poked her tongue out as far as possible to the sightless Maggie, and skipped off into the street. Instead of the beating which she expected next day, she found her mother burning her beloved book. Emma felt hatred rise within her. Murderous, in fact. What was she to do? It was "No" to reading, "No" to playing with boys, little children should be seen and not heard, "No" to sitting to a school scholarship. A hand brushed over her eyes if she looked at her elders too long. She felt like the rat that had been caught in a trap in Alfie Hill's back yard. She would do something about it when she could.

But in the meantime she had to grow up. And during that time her mother married again. The war continued. Uncle Reg had died from drinking too much beer, she had been told; Aunt Maggie and

Uncle George remained. George Green, her stepfather, was a small, thin, white-faced man. He liked his drink as her father had done, but her mother was wise this time and accompanied him on all his evening jaunts. He was employed in the council sewage works, and his wage was good. Aunt Maggie now had Reggie's room, and Emma the large front room upstairs. She still awoke frightened as she used to do, but Uncle George had told her to go to Auntie Maggie, who seemed to like her company now that the new stepfather had come. They both began to talk about the books that Emma had read, and the new Mrs Green was content that her daughter should read to the blind woman, and so take some of the responsibility of entertaining her off her hands.

And so during the next few years Emma read all the local library could offer her: Dickens, Jane Austen, the Brontës, Ethel M Dell, Kipling and so on. The Bible became of interest to her, and gradually Emma began to read this too. She found Auntie Maggie quite intelligent, as she would offer a great deal of comment on various books. So for a while Emma hastened home from school, did the errands and the household jobs allotted to her, always spurred on by her eagerness to go to Aunt Maggie's room and read. Life seemed rather pleasant because living was easier.

Growing up was a very slow business for Emma. From always living with elderly people she had developed into a very knowing, perhaps cynical, person; she was a dreamer too, and enjoyed spinning fantasies around herself. At fourteen she was by no means tall, perhaps five feet, two inches; but she was shaping well and showed signs of a strong personality. Her thick black hair she wore in a plait which hung well passed her waist. She had hazel-green eyes that were large and heavily lidded. These she learned at a very early age to use to her advantage. Her mouth was well-shaped, not too small, and covered a set of strong white teeth. But her skin was her most beautiful feature, flawless, with a bloom on it that was delightful to behold.

She still preferred the opposite sex as companions; indeed, she never made an intimate of any young girl. This preference was often viewed with suspicion by her mother, and consequently Emma's conduct grew rebellious. Later, virtue and honesty were to be the subjects of many arguments.

During the next two years Emma had various jobs. She was unsettled in her home life and was always planning in one way or another to leave home, but she found her mother very unsympathetic to her needs.

Suddenly, her sister Ruth reappeared in her life. Mother had been visiting a friend in a nearby town and on the return journey had met Ruth on a tram stop. Greetings were exchanged, and Ruth had agreed to come home the following week to meet her stepfather and renew her relationship with Emma. On this particular day, arriving home from work where she wrapped soap in a soap factory, Emma saw a young woman of about thirty-five seated at the table drinking tea.

"Emma," said her mother as she poured tea for her, "this is Ruth, your sister, come to see you."

"Hello," said Emma indifferently, hardly glancing at her long absent sister. "I'm in a hurry, Mother. Can I have something to eat right now because I want to go to the pictures, and they start at six-thirty!"

"Ain't you staying in?" demanded her mother sharply, "'Cause it's such a long time since Ruth came home, and just to say hello ain't enough."

"No. I'm not," snapped back Emma. "I made my arrangements to go out last week, and just because Ruth decides to come home is no reason for me to stay in. It's a pity she stayed away so long, and for all I care she can keep away."

"You little bitch!" cried Mrs Green, snatching Emma by the hair with one hand and giving her a resounding smack across the face with the other. "Boys. That's your trouble. Off with the boys every night, you dirty little slut!"

Ruth, who had been silently sipping her tea, rose quickly and in a quiet voice said, "I'm sorry I came, Emma. It was always like this when I lived at home, if home I could ever call it. I only agreed to come here on the spur of the moment. I was sorry afterwards, but I suddenly felt I'd like to see you because you were such a dear little baby and you were always with me when I was here." Turning to her mother Ruth said, "I'll go now. Don't have any more arguments over me. Let Emma go to her pictures and I'll make arrangements to see you all another time."

And from that day sprang a love, deep and sure, between the two sisters. It lasted for thirty years, Emma was loving, tempestuous creature that she was, Ruth the calm haven into whose arms she flew when life was difficult. Over the years Ruth gave Emma the love she would have given her own child if she had ever been fortunate enough to have one. But her marriage was barren. She gave Emma understanding, sincerity in her opinions, candid criticism, and steadfast loyalty.

The year was 1924, and Emma had been staying with Ruth for a week-end, a habit that had developed over the years. Emma would have liked to live with Ruth and her husband, Tom, but Ruth would not encourage it because she knew exactly what trouble this would cause for all involved. Instead, she made a warm welcome for her young sister whenever she came, and wisely advised her, "Let me talk to Mother, Emma, about you getting a job away from home. You could go into service, and I'm sure you'd really like it."

"Thanks," said Emma " but I don't want to be a skivvy."

Yet by a strange coincidence that was exactly what she did do. At the time she was working in a small bookbinding firm in Queen Victoria Street. Work was very slack, and on this particular day the young employees had been told not to return after lunch. Emma walked towards Ludgate Hill, not wishing to return home until the normal time, and hopped on the first bus that came along. She went upstairs to enjoy the open-air ride, and when the conductor called out "Fares please", she said "where does this bus go?" "Baker Street," was the sharp rejoinder, and Emma promptly took a ticket for there.

The day was warm and delightful. Little leaves gaily tripped along the gutter. People were leisurely walking up Fleet Street gazing into the offices of national papers. Emma had never been this way before and she was fascinated by the beautiful architecture of St Clememts Dane, the temple, and the little shops that looked exactly as if they had come from one of Dickens' books. For the first time she saw the Gaiety Theatre, caught a glimpse of the Lyceum, Charing Cross and on and on until at last she heared the conductor call "Baker Street, `ere for Baker Street." Down and on to the pavement went Emma, fascinated by so much movement. She caught sight of herself in a plate glass window, and thought how shabby she looked. She read notices on doors and in the windows of shops. "Servants' Agency" read one, "Many Vacancies, no charge, enquire within." Before she knew it, Emma was in a large office standing before a desk where a superior-looking lady sat. A notice "Enquiries" was displayed near her right hand. Keeping Emma waiting for a few seconds she finally condescended to ask, "Yes. Can I help you?"

Emma stared, tongue tied. So the young woman, with the flick of her hand indicating another desk with another person in occupation, "Parlour maids over there", and dismissed her.

The older woman seemed kind, and enquired if Emma was in a job, or out of work.

"Oh, I'm working, thank you very much," replied Emma. "I was passing, and curious, so I came in."

"We have one or two vacancies for under-parlour maids, and if you sit over there," continued the woman, indicating a vacant chair beside a pianola where a woman sat preparing to play it, "I'll see if we can fix you up."

Bewildered, Emma took the seat. A cup of tea with biscuits was placed into her hands, and the pianola began to play. Half an hour must have passed before she was called to the desk. People, both men and women, had been coming and going. Now and then a very elegant lady entered and talked with people. Emma assumed it was a would-be mistress interviewing a servant.

"I've just had this call from Wilton Crescent, Belgravia, for an under-parlour maid," said the clerk. "You'll be interviewed by the secretary, Miss Grant. The wages are £22 per year, uniform all found, a fortnight's holiday a year. In case you don't know the way, take a bus from here to Hyde Park Corner. Anyone will direct you from there. Your fare will be twopence, the secretary will give it you. There's no charge from us to you should you be engaged; employers pay engagement fees." And as an after thought, "The name of the family? Ah,yes, I almost forgot! Harkness - Lord and Lady Harkness."

Emma stepped out into the street and, still in a whirl, carried the instructions. Within half an hour she found herself mounting a short flight of marble steps to the front door of No 3 Wilton Crescent. She stood glazing at the big black knocker and a brass push bell, unable to decide which to use to announce her arrival. Suddenly the door gently opened and a man in a dark suit said, "Are you from Hunter's, the Agency? Please come this way."

Emma, quite tongue-tied, followed him into a huge hall with a black and white marble floor; a most magnificent staircase faced her. The balustrade was wrought iron with a broad mahogany rail. Emma thought the man leading the way was Lord Harkness himself. He opened a huge door and indicated that she should enter, then quietly closed the door and she was alone.

"Am I dreaming?" she thought, her feet sinking into a thick blue carpet. "Should I sit down?" she asked herself. Better not, because the armchairs of crimson brocade looked so deep she would not get up in time if anyone entered. So instead she walked across the room, looking and admiring the book-lined walls. The heavy door noiselessly opened and a little woman entered, and just as quietly closed it, saying as she advanced,

"Good afternoon. Do please be seated," indicating a hugh armchair. Timidly Emma sat on the very edge and waited. "I'm Miss Grant," the woman continued and, drawing an occasional chair near, went on, "Tell me about your previous positions and why you wish to leave your present one and come here."

Emma, who was really spellbound by the whirl of events of the afternoon, swallowed hard and, looking straight at Miss Grant, replied, "I have never been in service, Miss, only in factories. But I thought I would like to get away from factory life and have a complete change."

Miss Grant was silent for a moment. "Are you sure this kind of work would suit you? Do you know anything about parlour work? Your freedom would naturally be restricted. You will have only one half day a week, and one Sunday in four off duty."

A strange feeling came over Emma, a sense of potent unreality. A servant she would be, but if this room was an indication, she would be among beautiful surroundings. Everthing would be changed. It would be a new life. She could leave home, get away from her sharp-tongued mother, the house with its crumbling walls, the small back-yard and the shared privy. Here she could read, no doubt; it looked as though everybody in this house would always be reading with so many books about. Miss Grant cleared her throat, an indication that she was awaiting a reply.

"I would like it," said Emma. "I dislike my work and I want a complete change." How well she was lying, because up to this time of getting off that bus in Baker Street she had never disliked the work at the bookbinders. True, she had wanted to get away from home, but only to live with Ruth.

"How old are you?" was the next question, and the quick reply "Eighteen" was readily accepted, although she was just seventeen.

"When could you come to us?" Again came the quick answer, "This time next week."

So there, within a few hours, Emma or fate had made a quick change in the course of her life. As she left the house, she realised how much she had to straighten out before she could return. Walking across the gardens in the centre of the road she gazed at the beautiful house where she was to live. Maybe she would be a servant, but not always. Things kept changing. She had gained proof of that today. So, back to Ruth who would listen and advise.

Ruth was not too enthusiastic, as Emma had expected. It would have been much better if their mother had been told first, and Ruth found it difficult to believe that it had all happened on the spur of the moment. But after many arguments and promises always to go home on her days off, Emma, with her little tin box, finally found herself installed in the servants' quarters of No 3 Wilton Crescent.

Quick to observe and learn, she found the superior-looking person who answered the door to her was the butler, James. Then she met Henry, the footman, and Williams, the parlour maid. There were four housemaids, the senior being called Mrs Jakes, a cook and two kitchen maids, and June the tweeny maid with whom Emma was to share a room.

Her uniform was a blue print frock for morning, and a black dress with a white lawn apron, collar and cuffs for afternoon. In the morning she would wear a white mop cap; in the afternoon a large black bow. The French lady's maid offered to alter the dresses, for Emma was slim and much shorter than her predecessor. She soon grasped her duties and settled in very well. She learned that the family was quite small: Lord and Lady Harkness, and their only child, Miss Diane. They were at present holidaying in Venice, and would be back the following week. The staff appeared to have a warm regard for the family - -they had been cleaning and preparing the house ready for its owners' return, but as the chauffeur remarked, "I bet we shall only be here about a week before we go down to `Dene Hatch', the country residence."

The day the family returned, the whole house became alive. The telephone rang constantly; there were voices murmuring above the staff stairs, bells in the staff sitting-room were ringing, and Emma was fascinated to see various round discs in the wall indicator flutter to show for which room the bell was sounded. During dinner that night she was permitted to watch proceedings from the still room, and each time the door opened into the dining-room as Henry or Williams served the food, she could see Lady Harkness at one end of the table, Lord Walter Harkness at the other, and on his right his daughter Diane. Lady Harkness looked superb in a black velvet evening dress, with something very beautiful glittering on her ample bosom, her pure white hair, and diamonds in her ears.

She was about fifty years of age; Lord Walter was a little older, and his handsome shoulders fitted well into his dinner jacket. His hair, unlike his wife's, was thick, straight and black with a deep parting. But the daughter was the most beautiful; her hair was chestnut, and curled closely against the nape of her neck. Emma saw later that her eyes were a heavenly blue, and that she was slim and not too tall. She wore no jewellery. Involuntarily, Emma put her hand to her own hair and felt the coil of thick black hair which had been arranged to suit the bow, and wished hers looked as beautiful.

Henry shared many of his duties with Emma, and very soon his spare time too. They enjoyed the radio together and Henry would talk of the time when he had been a steward on board a ship. Sea sickness, which attacked him on each trip, had eventually forced him to take his present job. He was about twenty-four years of age, and quite experienced where girls were concerned. Not that he talked about his past affairs, but Emma easily sensed the kind of life he had lived. He had a way of brushing his hand across her lap if they sat together on the couch, and if he met her on the back stairs he would only make sufficient room for her to pass and their bodies would make contact. Emma was aware of all this, but she enjoyed the indulgence of a mild flirtation.

Chapter Two

Almost a month had passed since Emma had taken up her position in Wilton Terrace. She was willing, and pleasant to everyone above and below stairs. Diane had begun talking to her whenever she came into the library to tidy up the bookshelves. Diane was interested in languages and was quite a linguist. She had been commissioned by a well-known publishing firm to translate some French literature. She was watching Emma as she stood before a shelf, arranging a set of books in numerical rotation.

"Do you like reading, Emma?"

Emma nodded, "Yes miss, very much, but up to now I haven't had the opportunity to do so, very much."

"Well, help yourself whenever you wish. I'm sure my mother will agree, as long as it doesn't interfere with your duties."

With widened eyes Emma gave her swift reply: "Thank you, miss. I'll be very careful." A half smile flitted across her face as she turned again to the shelves. "I can learn a lot if I try," she thought and, raising a hand above her head, she took down a volume of The Works of Shakespeare. "May I have this, miss?" she asked, approaching Diane.

At that moment the door opened and James the butler entered with a card above a salver, handing it to Diane, who replied "Tell him to come in, James." And to Emma she smiled, "Thank you, you may take the book."

Feeling somewhat crestfallen Emma left the room, but not too late to see the newcomer - a tall, auburn-haired young man with piercing blue eyes. He looked down and saw a pair of enquiring eyes looking into his.

He went forward with outstretched hands, "Hello, Di - new maid?"

Impulsively Diane kissed his cheek, ignoring the question. "John, it's ages since we met! How are you, darling?"

His hands dropped on her shoulders. Drawing her close and kissing her with fervour, he said, "It's been far too long, darling, but now you're back we shall have to make up for lost time."

She looked at him, but did not reply. Something in his manner had changed. It was a subtle change, yet it was there all the same. A sudden fear came over her. "I think maybe we should make a break for good," she said. "I thought going away with my parents would help." She lifted her eyes to his. "Darling, you'll never get a divorce, and I can't go on pretending all the time. I hate this hole-in-the-corner business - meeting in small hotels, eating in wayside places, taking a taxi, being dropped in a district where I'm unlikely to be known and then you picking me up. It was all very beautiful at first. But I want more than stolen hours and odd week-ends. I want to be married to you, run your home, have your babies."

"We've talked this over before many times, Diane, and I've never led you to believe things would be any different from what they are." Drawing her close to him, he soothed her. "Be quiet, darling. Let's continue this way. It's the only way."

"Not for me, John." She walked across the room and lit a cigarette. "While I've been abroad I've given quite a lot of thought to our association, and I've come to realise that if you loved me as you've so often told me, you'd go to Lydia and make a clean breast of the whole situation. I have every reason to believe that she would agree to the divorce, especially as she no longer lives under your roof. She's been indiscreet on occasion, too, as you well know."

"What you say is perfectly true. Lydia and I long ago realised we couldn't live together, but divorce is another question. Under the terms of my grand-father's will I lose my inheritance if I either divorce or am divorced by my wife. Lydia's wise, she'll hang on to me because, without my inheritance, I'm penniless." His voice was steady and gentle. "I love you, Diane. I'm a selfish beast to ask you to continue the way we are, but to me it's the only way."

He drew close to her once again. She realised what he said was true. She loved him so very much, she could not elude him, and she relaxed in his arms. The fragrance of her beautiful soft hair intoxicated his senses, his dazzled brain could think of little else other than that she was his. Arguments could be averted to an embrace.

"Do you wish to escape me? I can't waste your life and mine - just waiting." His voice was none too steady. "Darling, darling Diane, please continue to love me."

She knew she would have many moments of regret. She knew she would continue to deceive her parents; but she also knew she loved him beyond all else. Giving him up, parting, she would lose what she regarded as wonderful and lovely and precious.

With a deep sigh, she said, "John, I love you. I'll often have moments of regret and discontentment for the real things I desire, but I love you and can't part from you." And then with a bright smile she said, "I'll ring for tea and tell you about our holiday."

As Emma and Henry brought in tea, Diane was saying, "Italy's really beautiful all the time, but I enjoy it more in the spring. The climate's not too hot, and my parents enjoy it then too. We met several interesting people in Rome, spent a few days with the Bottaras in Florence, and then joined the Tombolini family in Venice. It was there that I met the French publisher, Toulouse, who'd been told about my knowledge of foreign languages. He offered me the job of translating some French novels into English for Caldwells, who were considering the English publications. I felt flattered, and the salary's quite good, so I readily accepted. I will of course, have to pop over to Paris often for various discussions, and that's the main reason, John, why I'm here today and not with my parents at 'Dene Hatch'. You know they love London and really enjoy the various trips they make abroad. But really, they're only truly happy when they're down at 'Dene Hatch'. They're country folk at heart."

Emma followed Henry from the library with a thoughtful expression. She had noted the change in Diane when Sir John Seville had arrived. She sensed the feigned lightness of the conversation, and the strained air of both Diane and John as she and Henry arranged tea. She thought the atmosphere had been somewhat electric prior to their entry.

Entering the servants' hall, Henry caught Emma quickly to him and, with deliberation, pressed his lips firmly over hers. The suddenness of it caught her by surprise. The little shivers down her spine were exquisite. Henry held her closer, her arms round his shoulders, passion swamping their better judgement. Then, as she grew more aware of his seeking hands, Emma struggled to free herself.

"Henry! Not here, please."

And he: "Where, then?"

At that moment, some of the staff entered the room for tea and both tried to show composure, Emma hoping that no one had noticed how dishevelled her hair looked.

For some days Emma did her best to avoid being alone with Henry, but she knew that he was watching and waiting for the opportunity to be alone with her. That time came when, thinking Henry had gone out for his half day, Emma hastily went into the staff room after supper to read, and found him sitting there waiting for her. They were alone; the butler and parlourmaid were in their respective rooms, and the other maids in various parts of the house doing their evening duties.

"Hello, Henry," she said calmly, taking a seat at the other end of the room and opening her book as though to read. "I thought you were out, at the cinema or visiting your parents."

"I've hung around all afternoon waiting for this opportunity to be alone with you," he replied, getting up and sitting beside her. "What's the matter, Emma? Why are you avoiding me?" Taking her hand within his two he said, "I'm quite serious about you. You've tormented me ever since you came. I'm falling in love with you I think."

"Nonsense, Henry. The whole thing happened because we were both aware of something wrong between Miss Diane and Sir John. Anyone with half an eye could see <u>that</u>, and it fired our imaginations too. You may be serious about me, Henry, but only for one thing - sex. I would just be another of many conquests. I like you very much, but not enough for what you want of me. No doubt you find me outspoken, but where I come from, we are."

"But you responded, and if we hadn't been interrupted you would have agreed," was Henry's somewhat angry reply.

"Thank goodness we were, and now I know that, nice as you are, you're not for me. Nor, for that matter, I for you." Withdrawing her hand and rising from her chair, she walked towards the door. "Goodnight, Henry. Forget it, and let's be good friends."

Days passed, with Diane working hard and looking none too happy. She had suggested to Emma that after her evening duties she should sit in the library reading. It would be company, she said, with her parents away, and most of her friends still out of town.

The staff began to regard Emma with suspicion when they knew of the arrangement, and if it were not for those beloved books, Emma would have felt their disapproval more keenly. But she was learning all the time. She listened carefully to Diane when she spoke; she watched the graceful figure crossing the room; the way she sat down; how she handled the staff; and how, with graciousness, she got the maximum from them, without them being aware of it. Oh yes, Emma was learning, learning fast. Sir John was a frequent visitor to dinner and stayed quite late. On those occasions Emma would resume her rightful place below stairs.

Usually Lord Walter only needed one maid and the head kitchen maid to attend them at 'Dene Hatch', but he had some business acquaintance staying with him to discuss a contract with a Spanish firm in Madrid. As Manager of Electrical Engineering Proposals, Lord Walter enjoyed entertaining in his country residence. Henry and William had therefore gone to join the others, which left James and Emma in charge of the dining-room. James retired fairly early, leaving Miss Jakes to lock up. He was a very keen follower of horses, and betting was more than a hobby for him. Within the precincts of his chamber, he studied form for the next day, with the help of a little from 'the bottle'. At least, that was what Henry had reported to Emma.

So on the nights Sir John came, Emma became rather lonely. Cold-shouldered by the staff, she could hardly enter into their amusements, so she went early to bed with a book.

This night was hot and sultry, as is often the case towards the end of August; and looking at the sky, Emma hoped there would not be a thunderstorm. Jane came up to bed about eleven o'clock, and said, "There's going to be a storm. My word, it's hot. Do you mind if I open the curtains?"

"Not a bit. I wish my bed was further away from the window as yours is. I'm very nervous of thunder."

"Won't hurt you," said Jane, "Gee, my sister is the same, and when she was home, I always got into her bed when she was frightened. We soon consoled each other, though."

Closing her book and asking Jane to switch out the light, Emma said, "Goodnight, Jane."

Sleep came very quickly, and dreams, too. The storm gathered closer, and became violent. A terrific burst wakened her, and with a startled cry Emma jumped from her bed. All the old terror of her childhood enveloped her: the dark vivid flashes, the rolling thunder, the dreaded unseen surrounded her until, with a little whimper, she went across to Jane's bed, touched her, and said, "Jane, are you awake?" just as she would have said, "Uncle George, are you awake? I'm frightened." Sleepily, Jane drew her into her bed and comforted her shivering body by encircling her waist.

"It's all right, Emma. It's passing." But at that moment came a bursting of the heavens, so terrific that Emma felt all had ended; the walls must have fallen apart. She clutched fiercely at Jane, burying her head in Jane's ample bosom, trembling and speechless.

Gradually the tempest passed, and in the warmth of Jane's bed she fell asleep. She was again dreaming of the countryside. She was going to meet Ruth; they were to picnic; when suddenly a man on the horizon came towards her; they drew nearer each other; she couldn't see his face his head was downcast, but his steps were quick and eager. She too was drawing nearer with reluctant steps and then, face to face, she saw clearly now - it was Henry. He reached for her, he kissed her throat. She struggled, he kissed behind her ear, a hand seeking, as before, seeking first her breast, then across her stomach, confident; and she was falling to meet his passionate desires, and then a repulsive shudder shook her, and she screamed, "No! No!" trying hard to tear herself away, and a voice, a woman's voice was suddenly saying, "Be quiet, Emma. It's quite all right, darling," and the dream passed, and she was awake, and it was Jane who had soothed her with words; and it was Jane, not Henry. A wave of repulsion swept over her. Jumping from the bed she turned and smashed her fists into Jane's face and body. "You rotten, filthy, bitch!" she screamed. "I could kill you for this!"

"What's all the fuss about?" and cried Jane angrily, who was trying to hold her back, "I thought you'd like me loving you; it always calmed my sister. I told you." And then more calmly, she cajoled, "Emma, be quiet. Someone will come and there'll be such a fuss."

"Let them," replied Emma, "I'll tell them about you! You! A woman" And sobbing bitterly, she went back to her bed, and for the rest of the night she stared into the room, thinking and trying to overcome the storm that was within her.

There was no question of any further communication between them. The experience had been very humiliating, and for some time Emma felt unclean, and a certain amount of hatred sprang up for her own sex. She asked the Head Housemaid if she might change her room, and without much ado, she was given a tiny box-room away up in the attics, next door to Cook, who each night unknowingly gave comfort to Emma as she prepared for bed, by singing quietly to herself. It would often be terrifying to sleep alone, Emma knew, but she woud be comforted, she felt sure, if she repeated the Lord's Prayer - it nearly always worked.

As the days went by, Emma did try to cure herself, but she began to notice that something different was now urging her on; impulses never experienced before, desires unknown, were making her aware of herself. Emma was growing into womanhood. Men she now viewed with a different eye. She enjoyed the admiring glances as she went to and fro; her eyes, the best feature she possessed, she used to their best advantage; from now on she trained them to say more than her lips would ever utter. Oh, yes, Emma was well awake!

Diane had gone abroad again. Paris, James had said, and Emma felt rather hurt that Diane had not told her. Of course, it was impertinent of Emma to expect to be told of every move just because of the kindness Diane had shown her, but nevertheless she did feel upset.

She was taking some books back into the library one day when she heard the ring of footsteps behind her. Turning, she saw Diane and, amazed, nearly dropped the books.

"Oh, miss!" cried Emma, surprise and pleasure lighting her face, "I thought you'd gone away," she opened the door and stood aside for Diane to enter.

"I've been making arrangements to go to Paris, and have been down to `Dene Hatch' to my parents," said Diane. "I came back especially to see you. Will you close the door?" Emma still stood on the threshold. "And sit here by me. I want to talk to you."

A crowd of thoughts rushed into Emma's mind. "What have I done? Am I being sent away? Gosh, whatever is it? Surely I haven't offended anyone. I know I have a lot to learn, but I do try."

"You may know," Diane began, "that I work for a French publishing house. It appears my work is very satisfactory. I like it and it's been suggested that I take up residence for a while in Paris, and work in closer contact with Monsieur Toulouse. I'm well over 21 years of age, but my parents still consider me juvenile. I'm extremely fond of them, and don't wish either to argue or hurt them by being defiant. They suggested Miss Grant, but Miss Grant was once my nanny, and when I went away to school she became a companion and secretary to my Mother. I feel if she came with me she'd be treating me as a child again. Anyway, they insist that I have a companion. I've got a lot of friends, but I'm sure none of them would care to take on the job; they're inundated with engagements. So I've thought the matter over very carefully and suggested to my parents that I might take you. My Mother says that she knows very little about you but has got good reports of your work from Miss Grant. My father says you're too attractive to be in Paris without a companion yourself, but I've overridden their undue concern and, if you want and your parents will consent, I'll make arrangements for our departure two weeks from now."

As far as Diane was concerned the whole matter was settled. Emma was speechless, stunned that anything like this could happen to her. She asked for time to go home and get consent, and the first person she went to was Ruth. Ruth listened very quietly, and was a little pessimistic.

"Will you be safe, Emma? You don't know the language, and the foreigners will frighten you; and talking of fear, what about at night and in a strange place?"

"Oh, don't ask me soppy questions, Ruth," came the quick reply. "I just thought if I came to you, you'd come with me to Mother, and sort of back me up."

"Back you up? I can't back you up about something I know little about. I'd like to meet these people and try to form some sort of opinion."

"You can't do that! They're my employers and I don't want to offend them. Now don't you get offended," Emma added as a shadow of annoyance passed over Ruth's face. "You must try to understand that I'm telling you this is a wonderful chance for me. I can look after Miss Diane as well as any. She's not a difficult person at any time, and it will also be a great chance for me."

Ruth began to look convinced by Emma's apparent earnestness, and after she had changed her dress, she agreed to go to their mother and help smooth out the difficulties she knew would arise.

Difficulties there were, and none very logical. Their mother was like an excited hen, talking and gesticulating in a most unintelligent manner. But Ruth, by now Emma's ally, was able to smooth out the situation, and reassured her mother. "It's the best thing that could happen to our Emma." She was downright glad when they were both able to leave.

As they waited for the bus that would take Emma back to Wilton Crescent, Ruth tried to give some advice, but Emma was not heedful. She had got her own way and now she felt rather irritated and wished the bus would come along. When it did, she gave Ruth a quick peck on the cheek and barely looked back. If she had, she would have seen the tears that brimmed over in the loving eyes of her sister as she turned away and stumbled along the homeward road.

But a new life was opening up for Emma. One by one she was cutting the ties of her old life, and she felt elated. Lord and Lady Harkness came up to London to talk over the arrangements with Diane. Emma was taken to Harrods and fitted out with clothes suitable for the position she was now to take. A hasty farewell to the staff, and they were in the car, with Diane driving to Dover.

Emma was at first tongue-tied, but Diane was a very easy, friendly person who soon put her at ease. She was delighted at the interest and eagerness which Emma showed about everything.

"I know, of course, Emma, that you've never been abroad before, but tell me, what kind of holidays did you take with your parents?"

"Holidays, miss?" was the incredulous question. "We never take holidays where I come from. The only holidays we had were in early September when my Mother kept me from school to go hop picking. We used to sleep in a little wooden hut, cook our food over an open wood fire, sometimes have a bowl of soup in the church army marquee which was for the use of hop pickers. From about seven in the morning until dusk we would pick hops. Everybody where I come from has to work. No work, no food. For a few years while I was at school we were so poor that I had free meals." Emma faltered and turned her head away, looking across the countryside.

"Go on, Emma," urged Diane. "I'd like to know more about you. We shall be together some time, so we must get better acquainted."

Emma continued. "Look, miss, this is Kent we're travelling through, and it was Maidstone we used to go to. Never in all my dreams did I dream of a world different from the one I lived in; that one day I should ride through Maidstone in a beautiful car, in lovely clothes, on my way to Paris. I'm afraid I might wake up and find this is also a dream."

"Oh, no, Emma. This is no dream. And just to prove that you are in a different and better world - at least I hope it will be - we shall have no barriers about our relationship. From now on, you drop the Miss. You will call me Diane."

"Oh, no, miss. Whatever would her Ladyship say? I really couldn't do it, miss." Emma was flabbergasted. In less than six months she had reached these dizzy heights, from factory girl to companion to a young lady of aristocratic birth, a young lady presented at court, entertained by the King and Queen at Windsor. Surely that was enough? To also call her by her christian name was too, too familiar. Emma knew her place.

"We shall worry about her Ladyship when we meet again. In the meantime, if I regard you as my servant, which, incidentally, I do not, you must respect my wishes and call me by my name. It'll suit us both very well - we'll be regarded as social equals, which I hope we soon shall be, and you'll have much more fun when you join me in my round of pleasures."

Emma just sat there feeling, but hoping she did not look, a clown. Diane took a hand from the wheel for a second, saying, "Cheer up, Emma. You'll enjoy it all, I'm sure. Here we are at the docks. I hope you'll be a good sailor." Emma's quiet "Yes, miss" was smothered under the noise of a hooter sounding from a boat coming in to dock.

Within a very short time Emma was settled into her new life. It had been late afternoon when they arrived in Paris, and her spirits had soared at the sight of the chestnut trees on the boulevards. It was so beautiful, and far beyond the expectations of her imagination. As she lay in bed, it was so exciting to hear the roar of traffic, so close it seemed as though it would enter her room. Diane had taken a service flat, and the first night they went down to the dining-room for dinner, Emma prayed that she would not make a fool of herself. The table they were given was right across the room. It seemed miles away from the entrance, and as Emma followed Diane she was aware of the elegant people who looked so completely at ease. The waiter handed her a menu written in small, unusual handwriting and she looked appealingly at Diane, who coolly ordered for them both. Emma was tense during the meal, the starched dinner napkin slipping continuously down her lap, and she prayed for some outward poise, as those around her possessed.

After dinner they took a taxi, and Diane pointed out many landmarks which were to become familiar to Emma. The taxi took them uphill and she saw in the sky the beautiful floodlit dome of the Sacre Coeur. It looked wonderful. They took a walk over the cobblestones. People were rather noisy here, and many languages were spoken. How exciting it all was! In the square were gathered artists, more than a dozen displaying their paintings beneath the glow of the coloured shaded lamps. Some were even putting a finishing touch to their work. The crowd pressed close, and murmurs of approval could be heard. One young artist was, with extreme skill, putting the final strokes to a charcoal drawing of an elderly lady posing close by.

Diane took Emma's arm. "We must go and find a taxi. I'm getting tired and you must be, too. We'll come back to Montmartre many times. I love having meals here."

"It's wonderful!" Emma smiled gratefully, "Wonderful." And so began a new life.

Chapter Three

Paris! Paris! City of enchantment! Nothing can replace a walk along its river bank, where almost all at once one imbibes the atmosphere of this romantic city. On an island, as it were, stands the Notre Dame; on the left bank is the University, on the right the City and beyond, the residential area. The Seine is charged with history and ancient glory, and in the distance is the Louvre and the Arc de Triomphe.

As Emma walked towards the Champs-Elysées a line of the poet Baudelaire, arose in her mind: 'The dying sun sinks to sleep beneath an arch.' Paris! How happy Emma was, breathing the air of Goethe and Balzac and daily enjoying the history of France. Lights were beginning to come on as she hailed a taxi and with confidence said, "Twenty-two Avenue Friedland." It was where she and Diane lived. Diane had by now given up the service flat and had taken over their present abode from a friend. Most of their meals they ate out, and when in no mood for that, Emma was able to provide whatever was necessary to eat. They had a daily woman who cleaned and washed for them. With their usual warmth and easy-going natural ways, Diane had quickly made Emma feel at ease, and now after six months together a warm friendship and understanding had sprung up between them. Emma had natural insight and with careful study, had acquired almost perfect poise and manner. She had to be careful with her speech at times, but was confident that eventually she would succeed.

Always perceptive, she soon established in her mind the arrangement between Diane and John Seville. He was a frequent visitor to Paris and their flat. Consequently she knew what was required of her, and readily made herself scarce on these occasions. By so doing she got to know Paris very well. It didn't bother her that she roamed alone, there were so much to see, so much to learn. She got to know the Latin Quarter. She would walk the Rue Claude-Bernard, looking in the second-hand book shops, mingling with the students who lodged around. She would visit churches, walk along the Quai

De Montebello, and enjoy the work of would-be artists. Then on, perhaps, to the corner of the Saint-Michel and Saint Germain Boulevards, to watch the steady flow of traffic, and so to the Louvre, where she had been that afternoon. She had sat on a little stone seat in The Throne Hall, picturing the scene of the marriage of Mary, Queen of Scots to the Dauphin, and had visualised the wax effigy of Henry IV which had lain in state until it was later replaced by the coffin. She tried to picture herself back in the fabulous past, taking part, perhaps, as a serving maid when the Louvre was a royal palace. She herself was the maid who carried a cloak, or shawl, or the fan of her queen, always attentive, always at hand. She was quiet and submissive, but knew at the right moment when to raise those beautiful eyes of hers, and for one fleeting moment catch the glance of the king. There were many favourites in court, and ere long she planned to be one. Riches would be hers, she would wear beautiful clothes, she would have many lovers, some would duel over her, and then she would meet the man for whom she would give up all in the name of love, and life for both would be a perpetual honeymoon. Emma sighed, suddenly aware of someone standing quite near, and a voice saying, "My word, you were miles away!" She blinked and, coming back to present day earth, answered, "I was dreaming. I believe I often do," and rising from her seat she looked up into the face of a young man, quite tall and fair.

"You spoke to me in English," she added. "How did you guess?"

"I didn't," he responded. "I heard you speaking to a guide some time ago. I've been looking at the works of Botticelli and Leonardo Da Vinci in the Long Gallery, but it's near closing time and seeing you with that far-off look as I came through, I felt I had to rouse you, although the bell which is going to ring in a few seconds would have served the same purpose."

"But not so gently," said Emma with a laugh as the 'all out' bell began to ring with deliberation.

They were now outside, and Emma was about to say, "I go in this direction", when he interposed. "I say, we're both English, and I know that doesn't give me the right to force myself on you, but I'd like to meet you again. Could we dine this evening, say eight o`clock? I could meet you wherever you like. I'm Andrew Craig, by the way. I'm from London and I can tell you more about myself this evening." It was as though he had already heard her acceptance, for he went on, "Shall we dine in Montmartre, and can I call for you?"

Without hesitation Emma said, "I live in the Avenue Friedland, number 22. My name's, Emma Greaves, and I'm companion to Diane Harkness, the daughter of Lord and Lady Harkness of Belgravia."

"Shall I call a taxi for you?" offered Andrew, and Emma replied, "No, thank you, I'll walk a bit of the way."

She did not wish to return too early, for John would still be with Diane.

And so by the time she had walked a while, hailed a taxi that took ages to free itself of outgoing traffic, it was well past six o'clock when she let herself into the flat. On the little hall table there was a note from Diane saying she was having dinner with John, but was going out beforehand to the Villa of Toulouse near Fontainebleau to discuss some work, and that she hoped Emma would not be too lonely.

Taking her bath and dressing leisurely, Emma was only just ready when the door bell rang. Not quite sure as to whether or not she should ask Andrew in, she opened it, but he had already made the decision. With one foot over the threshold he said, "I'm a little early. I hope you don't mind."

"Not at all," Emma replied, and with a little touch of the Cockney wit she would never lose, added, "It would be stupid of me to <u>ask</u> you to come in!" Closing the door she led him into the sitting-room. "Pour yourself a drink. I'd like a little brandy." She went into her bedroom to get her wrap. When she returned, he was standing by the window, looking on to the road. She thought how tall and nice he looked, fresh and clean. Her eyes travelled over his dark, immaculate suit, his snow-white linen; she noted the line of his fair, wavy hair that met the broad brow, and the long sensitive fingers as he handed her the brandy.

Picking up her wrap, he folded it across her shoulders, admired the beautiful texture of her skin, the coil of lovely black hair in the nape of her neck, the clinging black dress on her well-proportioned form, and the dark line that divided her bosom; but what attracted him most of all were her eyes, large, soft, and luminous. They seemed to say so much, and yet remained mysterious. It had been the same that afternoon.

"Shall we go?" he said.

They found a table at the Auberge de la Cremaillere, its background music played by some Russians. To Emma it was not important that she ate, but that here she was in Paris, enjoying life, with a most charming escort.

He told her that he had a flat in Eaton Square, was interested in art, and often came to Paris. In a few weeks he was going to Florence to meet some friends and perhaps stay with them a while. He said he was twenty-six, had parents and a brother two years younger than himself. He was interested in sport and took a lively interest in cricket. He said he had a private income which kept him in comparative comfort, but his father was always hoping that he would enter the family business of Craig & Sons, Wine Importers. He had been educated in the usual way, Winchester and Oxford. He had a blue for cricket, and had travelled quite a bit. "Now you tell me about yourself, Emma," he said, putting a hand over hers as it lay on the table between them.

"There's little to tell," she said, "nothing that's worth repeating." She briefly related her childhood, up to the present.

"How old are you?" he said.

"Twenty," was the hearty reply, hoping he did not discover she was lying. People always accepted what she claimed about her age, and Ruth said she looked older than she was.

I don't suppose you're married?" was Andrew's next question.

"Oh, no. Are you?"

He paused, while he looked at her rather searchingly. In a rather quiet tone he said, "We've known each other for only a few hours, and this is not the time for confidences." Calling the waiter, he added, "Shall we go for a walk?"

Emma felt rather crestfallen as she left the restaurant, but decided that after all it was to much too expect that they should tell each other their life stories. And anyway, they might never meet again. "Enjoy the evening, Emma," she thought.

Hand in hand they approached the terrace of the Sacre-Coeur, and they were both exhilarated by the happy atmosphere of the city. Around them was a galaxy of stars, and gradually they could distinguish from those in the heavens the Opera Comique, Boulevards, Eiffel Tower and others. It was as though Paris were beginning to awaken, as if she were drawing aside the curtain of sleep, and shadows were disappearing. Pleasure-loving foreigners were entering the cabarets and night clubs. Andrew and Emma stood hand in hand, watching. He, of course, had seen it many times before, but this was the first time Emma had stood watching the night-life of Montmartre with such a wonderful companion. She trembled a little, and drawing her nearer he said, "You're cold. We'll go down to the square for a drink."

It was around two in the morning when they went down the Flight of Steps and hailed a taxi. He was still holding her hand when she approached the flat, which was in complete darkness. He took the key as she drew it from her bag, and opened the door. Hesitant and uncertain, Emma said, "I'm not sure if Diane's home. Would you care for a last drink?"

And he replied, "No, thank you. I've enjoyed this evening immensely and I'll ring you in a few days'time." Taking her hand, he held it for a second, then brushed her cheek with his lips; then, before she could thank him, he was gone.

Closing the door and entering her bedroom, Emma mused about the evening's adventure. She hoped they would meet again, he was so charming. They hadn't talked very much, yet she knew they had enjoyed each other's company; the silence between them had been as intimate as conversation. There was a quality about him that excited her. She hoped he would ring; she hoped he would say, "I must see you again, I must" - but whatever she hoped he would say was lost as she drifted into a dreamless sleep.

The next day was a dull, wet and dreary one. Diane and Emma had breakfast rather late, and it being Sunday, they were both considering the possibility of going to church. Looking out of the window and watching the driving drizzle of rain, Emma said,

"We can't walk to St.George's, Diane. I must call a taxi." But the peal of the door bell hastened her to admit John Seville.

"Good morning, Emma. I hope Diane's about," he said, rushing into the living-room. Emma went quietly out into the street, surprised at the sudden appearance of John Seville, and wondering a little.

He, meantime, was holding Diane by the shoulders. "I had to come back, darling. I couldn't sleep. What do you do to me that puts me in these black rages? I'm filled with shame and frustration. I torture myself that you no longer want me. My blood turns to fire in my veins; from you there is no escape, even if I wanted it. When I take you there's no response; you hold back; you won't give. You are my life, my existence. I can't think of the future without you."

Diane tried to free herself from his grasp, but he clung to her fiercely. This was the aftermath of a stormy evening. She had returned from Fontainebleau the previous day to dine with John, and then returned to the flat. She had again, as often in the past, referred to their relationship and her longing for the day when she would be his wife. She had suggested that he give up his inheritance, get a divorce, then a job, and marry her.

The usual excuses and arguments followed. She felt his will stronger and stronger. She had to try to resist him. He was pulling her down to nothingness. She had come to Paris, mostly to see him and be with him more often. Emma was an excuse, a cloak, a veneer of respectability. Their passions ran high, they were insatiable, and she was drowning in the fathomless flood of his possessiveness. Her life had been guided and secure up to the time of meeting John. It had run on an even keel. The ground had been firm beneath her feet, but now she floundered in quicksand, the quicksand of his passion - and finally she had said, "If you can't give me the security that I ask for, we must part. I'm not happy and I feel defeated." So saying, she had passed into her bedroom to remove her wrap. He had followed her and had flung her across the bed, kissing her and removing her garments piece by piece until she was naked. It was unforgivable, this nudity; she had struggled free as he'd tried to remove his own clothing, but he'd caught her at the door, and they had fought together like savages. She had bit him, he had flung her once again on to the bed and forcibly taken her. Her sobbing had been to no avail. Afterwards she had silently taken her robe, gone to the bathroom and locked the door. He had followed, tried the door, called to her to open it, and asked her forgiveness, but she had quietly said, "Go away, John. I never wish to see you again."

After a while he had left, and she had gone to straighten her room, thankful that Emma wasn't yet home.

She had heard Emma return and go to her room which adjoined hers. Diane lay staring into the darkness, her mind awhirl with thought of relationship with John. They had met the previous year at a houseparty and had been very attracted to each other. He was charming and attentive, they had begun to see each other quite frequently. She learned he was married but lived apart from his wife; and she knew that her association with him was getting out of hand. Her best friend, Veronica Bellman, had warned her that people in their set were talking.

"Talking about what?" demanded Diane.

"About you and John, Diane. He's married and not living with Lydia, and when a married man in those circumstances is seen about with another woman, tongues will wag."

"Let them wag," reported Diane. "There's no harm in our friendship, we enjoy each other's company, we like the same things."

Yet in her heart she knew it was completely innocent. Vaguely, she knew the time was at hand when he would no longer be satisfied with this platonic friendship. There was a yearning in her that had to be answered. The summer of that year slowly drifted away, and the golds and bronze of autumn began to appear. She had asked John, along with other young people, for a long weekend at Dene Hatch, and one evening, when they had finished coffee after dinner, the two had wandered into the garden together. The air was warm and the full moon hung in the beautiful clear sky. They wandered into the park, walking hand in hand until they came to the summer house. Without a word they went in, and lifting her on the settee he took her. Her cry of pain was drowned in the storm of his passion.

"Darling, darling Diane!"

"John, I love you!"

And again they sank into the swamp of their own passions. There was no tenderness between them at that moment, just a gratification of their insatiable desire, and when they were temporarily spent, they lay in each other's arms and he could see, as the moonlight glanced across her beautiful face, that he was the victor, that he had conquered. He would, from then on, discover the hidden beauties of her body, the maddening hidden places. He raised himself and leant over her, placing his hand on her hard nipple. His temples throbbed, desire gave in to reality - she lay there awaiting him. And when the maddening intoxication of the senses had been spent, and the moon was dimmed by the rising sun, they returned to the house, hand in hand as before.

So began their secret life. They tried not to be seen together by friends and acquaintances. They met in out-of-the-way places. He was happy, he had discovered her, he had found the secret beauty of her, he loved her from the crown of her head to each little toe. He took his pleasure often, and outwardly they were satisfied with each other. But he did not know her, the hidden one, who lay asleep inside that beautiful body.

They felt no shame in their relationship. They had created a togetherness that would have no end. He felt sure of that, even though their pleasures were unlicenced. But gradually the seed of discontent grew within her, and lying in his arms after the consummation of their love, she felt dissatisfied. He was not wholly hers. As he placed a hand upon her belly, two tears involuntarily oozed from beneath her eyelids. "Empty," her heartbeats said, "empty." No child to stir within her womb, no ultimate end of the passion and love that flamed, which, when dying, were aflame again. No movement here within her to tell her that his seed would live, would be flesh and blood, evidence to the world of their oneness. He kissed her, feeling and tasting the salt tears that slowly trickled down her cheeks.

"What is it? Why the tears? Have I done something to hurt you?"

How could she explain the crying need for his children? How could she explain to him? Her hand went to his head and grasped it. "No, no, I'm just a little excited." And so, gently, he kissed her, caressed her and loved her, but for her the zest had gone.

The months passed and Diane's love deepened. He, like the crowing cock, was prancing in his joy, his victory. He had no thought for any other future, he was content, satisfied. His manhood was justified.

They were motoring back from a secluded village in Somerset, and he was to drop her on the outskirts of London. The day was dull, and none too warm. She snuggled close to him, closed her eyes, and dreamed: dangerous dreams that would only bring discontent into their lives if she gave free reign to them. But the urge to speak was upon her; involuntarily the words toppled over her lips: "John, how lovely if we were going to our own home, and how wonderful if I could say to you that I was going to have a child, your child."

Suddenly the car swerved and he brought it to a halt in the lonely country lane.

"Don't ever speak that way again! We have each other. I love you more than words can say. You know all the difficulties." John was furious.

"Yes," she breathed, "I know them all." And added with a trace of bitterness, "If you love me as you say, why won't you get a divorce and marry me?"

"Diane, why suddenly all this? I believed you were happy. We've gone all over this, time and time again. You accepted it."

"Yes, John, we have gone over the only bit of excuse you give, with regard to your freedom from Lydia in the future, but you've never talked of wanting to marry me, giving me a home and a family. Perhaps you don't want these responsibilities, perhaps you like this kind of life - with me as your mistress, and the excitement of these clandestine meetings."

Violently he grasped her arms, and shook her as best he could in such a confined space. Fiercely, he said, "I love you, I would marry you, if I had sufficient income to keep you."

She drew away, despising him. "Take me back to London, John," she said, "You'll never marry me, but it's no use crying about it - is it?"

She had joined her parents in Italy to avoid him, and on that particular day when Emma had first seen John Seville, Diane had met him again and was determined to discontinue the affair. But once within his arms all resistance melted away. As he fondled her, his presence overwhelming, she was hot with desire for him, and she found herself again planning and meeting him in secret places. Toulouse, who had met her and offered work which she gladly accepted, had hinted that Paris was the right place to really get down to the translations. Diane had seized the suggestion eagerly, and found that by using Emma as companion, she could avert any suspicion about John and herself. They had been together in Paris for almost six months. He was insatiable, and at first her passions were as strong as his, fierce, sharp and sensual. Sheltered within his arms as he caressed her, all her resistance would melt away. She became nothingness and was lost.

But once alone she would think back to his cool reasoning, and little doubts would assail her. When he was away the hours would slowly pass, and gradually the longing to cease this tempestuous life with John began to form in her mind. In her very bowels was the longing for his children; to be together openly; to be acknowledged by the world. She had decided that night when she had travelled from Fontainebleau to join him for dinner, to talk with him and persuade him. Over dinner, he had been charming and she gay.

"Will we be alone when we get back to the flat?" he had enquired as he called the waiter for his cheque, and she had replied, "I can't say. Emma was out when I left this evening, but she knew we were dining together, and she always makes herself scarce then. Emma's a very nice person, and loyal too. She fully understands the situation, although I've told her nothing."

"Let it be hoped that she's comprehending tonight," he retorted. "I want to get you in my arms." Leaving the restaurant he hailed a taxi, and sat very close and silent beside her.

The flat was quiet, and Diane switched on the lights and drew the curtains. John snatched her to him, raining kisses on her eyes, her lips, her throat. His body seemed to melt into hers. She was enveloped with his desire and she responded - almost - but in the corner of her mind arose the doubts and fears, the desires of all women, and putting her hands to ward him off, she looked deeply into his eyes, eyes that were cold blue, but now aflame with desire.

"John, please listen to me, I love you and want you, but this artificial way of life is wearing me down. Please, darling, get a divorce and marry me."

"I've explained time and time again, darling, that it's impossible - we're both happy in our relationship. My desire and love for you will always be the same."

"Desire, yes, but love, I sometimes doubt. If you truly loved me you'd always want to be with me. You'd marry me and give me children, you'd work for me."

"I refuse to discuss it further," he cried angrily, and lighting a cigarette he walked away from her.

A sudden anger and disgust for him filled her very being; she wanted to inflict some hurt on him as he hurt her. She hated him at this moment. He was suave and contemptuous as he spoke to her, and rushing past him to her room, she flung over her shoulder those two fateful sentences: "If you can't give me the security I ask for, we must part. I'm not happy and I feel defeated." He had gone almost berserk; he had taken her like a wild animal, and then left her.

And now he was back, contrite, pleading, begging, imploring. The closeness of him, the nearness, the heat of his desires revealed the weakness of her revolt. He lifted her into his arms and took her again, all control abandoned - but for her the zest of his love-making was gone.

"Don't, oh, don't!" she cried. "Keep away from me!" and he, getting more insane with her rejecting, said, "I take what I want", and spent himself.

Her sobs were uncontrollable, and anger rose swiftly within him. His manliness was rejected; she would have none of him. Then no other man would have her; no other man would have this beautiful body, and know the beauty of her sex. She was his, these breasts beneath his hands, this smooth belly, the thighs that enveloped him.

He kissed them. "Mine!" he said, "mine!" and in his frenzy he looked into to her face, the eyes closed, a small frown between her level brows, the lips held firm and rigid.

"No other man shall caress her!" his tortured brain screamed out. "No lips shall cover the pulse that beats for me in that beautiful throat!" His hands passed over it, pressed it gently, firmly. A fluttering sound hovered over her and she was gone.

Chapter Four

Emma sat in the beautiful church of St George, and mechanically took part in the Sung Eucharist. She was not a confirmed member of the Anglican faith. Her mother's creed had been: "Those that don't go to church are better than them that do, at least they're not hypocrites." Sunday school had simply been a way of disposing of Emma for an hour, a means to a summer outing and a winter party. God to Emma was a Being who sat on a golden throne; When the time came to go before him, an angel with a book would read out your earthly misdeeds, and He would punish you accordingly. Also, whilst on this earth, Mother always said He had a way of punishing you too. And all through Emma's childhood she had feared him; that is what the Bible said, "Fear Him". But when she had grown older and began to think upon the wonderful things in the world, the beauty of so many of the Bible stories, the wonder of music, colour and sound, the creation of all living things, Emma also began to wonder at and love the Creator of them all. She enjoyed the times she attended a religious service. It gave peace to her heart, contentment to her mind, and she wished very much that she had someone to help her towards the kind of life where God, His teachings and His works would become part of it. Diane went to church at regular intervals, but Emma considered it all part of her upbringing and did not seem to bring much joy to her. Emma wanted something different. This morning, wet and dreary though it was, her heart was uplifted as she joined in the singing:

"O God unseen but ever near
Thy Presence may we feel ..."

Pure and clear her voice rose. She was unaware of its beauty. She just loved singing. And then, as she was on her knees while the congregation filed to the altar, the tears trickled down her cheeks for pure love of Him who was the Creator.

When she left the church she thought it best not to return to the flat. Instead, she hailed a taxi to the Luxembourg Gardens, which she and Diane frequented very often. Diane's french friends would idle a morning away sitting beneath the trees around the Medici Fountain. Here Emma hoped to meet someone she knew, but the watery rays of the sun had lured many people out. She sat down and waited. She closed her eyes, and no longer saw the statues of such people as Georges Sand, Hugo, Baudelaire and Banville. Instead she felt their presence and the presence of all those famous people who had in the past lived in the vicinity, and had been its most devoted admirers. She had read that the Florentine queens, Catherine and Mary de Medici, had made the Luxembourg and the Tuileries their contribution to the Parisian way of life. The park was now claimed by the Latin Quarter, a haunt for artistic people from all over the world. They enjoyed the autumnal sun that sat behind the golden trees and enveloped them in melancholy.

How long Emma sat there she was unable to say, not having a watch; but she imagined it was quite some time for her day dreaming always seemed to occupy many of her hours. She heard children playing quite near; she opened her eyes to watch them. They looked very poor children but they were having fun throwing the ball to one another; they looked happy little urchins, and swiftly Emma's mind drifted back to her own school days, the free meals, and the harshness of her childhood. Impatiently she rose to her feet, for such thoughts as these always made her angry, and she walked from the Gardens into the Boulevard St Michel. From there she entered the Boulevard St Germain and, going towards the Assemblee Nationale, sat at a table on the Boulevard of the Café De Flore. As she drank coffee and ate a croissant, the sun came out more brightly. There was a peaceful feeling around her, and somewhere not far away she could hear the gentle tinkle of water - a fountain perhaps. Nearby at another table sat a man with a pile of papers beside him. One in his hand was the London Daily Mail, and a mere sight of it caused a wave of homesickness to envelop her. She felt lonely, wanting to belong, to be in a happy family circle, not on the edge of someone else's. She was getting around as she always hoped she would; she had ideas and ambitions. Yet until now she had indeed been only a servant. And even now in a crowded room with Diane, she was alone; the larger the crowd, the more she felt her loneliness and lack of background. Mostly, people spoke to her only when they required something or were looking for Diane. But yesterday - or was it the day before? - she had met Andrew Craig, and she had hoped they could be friends. He had said, "I'll ring you in a few days", and she hoped he would. It was strange that he had evaded her question as to whether he was married or not. But, after all, it was quite reasonable that one should not lay bare all one's private life within an hour or so of meeting someone for the first time.

Now she had to return to the flat and see if Diane needed her, or if she had gone out with John. Somewhere in the distance a clock chimed two. Emma hailed a cruising taxi and shortly afterwards let herself into the flat. All was quiet, and she went into her bedroom humming a tune, flung her shoes off and lay for a few minutes on her bed.

"I do hope Andrew will ring me soon," she thought. How nice he was, what beautiful hands he had. She must tell Diane all about him. Perhaps Diane knew him, and if that were so Emma was confident at some time she would meet him. But enough of wishful thinking. Time for a bath. She undressed and put on her dressing gown. The flat was very still and an eerie feeling came over her. She chided herself for the fear that always beset her when she was alone. Briskly, she walked across to the bathroom door. It was ajar; she opened it wider, and across her path lay John Seville.

Rooted to the ground, Emma could only stare. She could not see his face. It was turned away from her. She saw he was only partly clothed. His socks were wrinkled about his ankles, his body dressed only in vest and briefs. Confusion entered her mind. She could not see from what lower region the blood had come; she could not understand what she saw. She called him by name, to no response. He was so still. She stooped and lifted the arm nearest the pool of blood. It was inert. She dropped it in horror. Blood stained her clothing now, and like a dart she ran into Diane's room.

The curtains were drawn and she rushed to open them. Turning, she was startled to see that all the flowers from the living-room had been taken and strewn upon the bed. She drew nearer, fascinated and yet petrified. Who on earth had brought the flowers in here? Timidly she put forth her hand to touch them, and then her vision cleared and she saw beneath them a shape. Swiftly she pushed the flowers aside, and saw Diane looking at her, a smiling Diane, the make-up on her face somewhat blurred, but not enough to tell Emma that for a few hours now she had been dead.

"Diane, Diane, what's the matter?" As her fingers touched the smiling, immobile face, the shrieks that came from her as her fingers sent the electric message to her brain were awful to hear, and Emma dropped to the floor in a dead faint.

When consciousness returned, and with it the full horror of all around her, she could not rise but crawled from the room to the hall door. With great difficulty she struggled to the lock and opened it, feebly crying as she did so, "Help me, Oh, help me!" But darkness and oblivion overcame her once again and she collapsed across the outer corridor.

Once again when she became conscious the horror of it all swept over her, but she was no longer alone. She lay on the settee in the living-room. It was now dark; all the lights were on, and the room seemed full of people. There were men in uniform. There was one in a dark lounge suit sitting at Diane's desk, and as the perplexed mist cleared from Emma's eyes she saw Monsieur Toulouse. He came towards her as her eyelids opened, touched her hand with a reassuring gesture and said, "How are you, Emma? Do you think you could tell us all about it?"

Another man who had been out of sight came towards her and felt her pulse. He must be a doctor, Emma thought.

He said (although she did not understand him), "This young girl must go to hospital and have a few days of complete rest. Then you can question her. As she is now, anything could happen to her brain, and then for the rest of her life she would most probably be in an asylum."

The man at the desk came over to join the conversation. "But we want to know all we can as soon as possible, doctor. We must go on with the case."

The doctor replied, "There is little to get on with, Superintendent. It is a clear case of murder and suicide, and this young person stumbled upon it. There seems now only the inquest to deal with. Monsieur Toulouse has telegraphed the parents of the dead woman. They should be here by tomorrow, and you found the man's address and sent a wire to his wife. It can clearly be seen that this was a crime of passion."

The Superintendent nodded in agreement. "True, true," he said. "When the young lady has been rested we will of course, require a statement. By the way," he said, turning to Monsieur Toulouse, "who is she? Does she live here?"

"Yes," was the reply, "Miss Emma was companion to Diane Harkness. She came with her from Lord Harkness' household, when Diane decided to live in Paris to be near my publishing firm while she translated some novels. She was an excellent linguist and I felt very privileged to have her work for me. It was only last night that she came to my home in Fontainebleau to discuss some work, but didn't stay too late as she had to meet John Seville. I knew vaguely of the love affair between them, but I feel sure that her parents didn't. I have often suspected that coming to live in Paris was a very good opportunity for them both to carry on this affair. For it to end this way is a great shock to me, for they appeared to be very normal, level-headed people."

Monsieur Toulouse stopped for breath. He was a short, thick-set man with thinning hair, about forty years of age but looking much older. He gesticulated all the time he was speaking, and Emma could see through half closed lids the flash of a diamond ring on his right little finger. He was filled with emotion and she felt that tears were not far away. Quietly, her brain began to dim and she felt herself drifting slowly away from the room. She was a little girl once again, frightened, rushing up to Uncle George, with eyes at every corner watching her, and hands outstretched to grasp her. Breathlessly she rushed into Uncle George's room. She was safe. She stood by the bedside. He was in bed. She was calling him, but he slept on. Fear caught up with her again. "Uncle George!" she screamed and probed him vigorously. He would not move, and in the moonlight which streamed across his bed, she pulled the clothes aside and, horror of horrors, she was looking at Diane, and Diane was smiling. Emma's hand was wet and sticky from the contact.

"It's blood!" she screamed, "It's blood!" And piercing screams rent the room.

Soothing words came to her. She was being lifted; people in white were hovering nearby. There was a short, sharp pain in one of her arms, and then oblivion.

How many days Emma had been in hospital she did not know, but it seemed that no sooner did she try to open her eyes than she was in darkness again. She was vaguely conscious at times that people were around her, talking about her, sometimes calling her by name, but she felt so much more secure with her eyes closed that they did not know if she was half feigning unconsciousness. To be quiet, not to talk, not to open one's eyes was so much better. She preferred it this way. But a voice that she loved seemed to penetrate her waking mind, and the hand that held hers was so reassuring that finally she opened her eyes a little.

Yes. It was true, it was - she was safe, secure and loved. It was Ruth, who was saying, "Dear Emma, It's me - Ruth. Look at me."

And look she did, and smiled too, saying, "Ruth! Am I all right? Am I safe?" and closing her eyes drifted into sleep, unconscious sleep.

It took weeks to bring Emma back to a healthy way of life. Ruth had been brought over by Lady Harkness, whose heart was torn between horror at the death of her beautiful daughter and the possibility of a permament break-down of Emma. It was Henry who said, when enquiries were being made amongst the servants about Emma's nearest relations, that he thought her sister Ruth would be the one who would best help. They had found Ruth's address, and Lady Harkness had requested Henry to take her to it. There had been many explanations and difficulties to overcome, but when Ruth realised how ill Emma was, she agreed to go to Paris. Her mother was too much of a rough diamond to set out on such a mission, and Ruth knew her very presence at the bedside would do Emma more harm than good.

For two weeks she remained at the hospital, spending as much time with Emma as the doctors thought fit. She was told to carry on normal conversations as though Emma could respond. It was difficult to find what to say. The little of life that Ruth knew, and all the roughness of the sisters' miserable childhood did not seem much to bring interest and encouragement to a girl with a mental break-down. Finally Ruth hit upon the idea of talking to Emma as she had when she was very little girl, and long before she had married Tom, her husband. She gently hummed their favourite songs; she told stories of Red Riding Hood and Cinderella. With an imaginary door she called 'Peep bo!', and each evening before she left sang the lullaby songs, "Golden Slumbers Kiss Your Eyes", and "Hush a bye baby on the tree top". Each evening Ruth would leave the little private room, downcast, feeling foolish and inadequate. Yet the doctors were full of hope and encouragement, and so Ruth continued with her childish games.

And then the reward came. Emma opened her eyes, smiled and, as the doctors said, drifted in to what they hoped would be a healthy sleep.

Now that Emma was progressing, Ruth thought that she must return to England. The very little she had seen of Paris was no inducement for her stay. She was a true Londoner of the East End, and it was only that part of the world that she ever wished to know or live in. It had been a great wrench for her to leave her home and husband. Her world consisted of a back street in Canning Town. She felt safe in the dockside, and enjoyed the market which was held in Rathbone Street, leading into Barking Road. That was as far as she had ever been since she had married, with the exceptions of the early days outing to Southend with Tom. It was very nice there, for the day; the atmosphere of the pubs and cockle stalls were similar to those at home. But when the day ended, it was always a relief to return home to the little house with its whitewashed step and lace curtains, held in place with wide blue ribbon. Ruth took pride in her little house. She longed now for the sight of these familiar things. The sounds of the ships' hooters, the gasometers in Becton Road, the coloured people that lived around her, the children playing and shouting in the road, and most of all, Tom, who was a 'boiler scurver' at King George V dockyard. She longed to be home to hear his key in the door when he returned from work, and she would open the kitchen door as he came down the passage, which was so dark, into the light. He was quiet and not demonstrative, but she knew he was always pleased to go home, and as he passed the door on his way to the scullery to wash, he would call out:

"Hello, mate. Won't be long. Pour my cuppa while I wash and change. It'll be ready to drink then."

And she would reply, "All right, Tom. Don't be long `cause I've got some good mussels for tea and the bread's still warm!"

In the autumn and winter he was content to sit by the kitchen fire, the stove bright from daily polishing, and the fender with "Home Sweet Home" stamped into it, reflecting the flames in its polished steel. From the local news and a national daily paper he would, from time to time, read out little bits of interest to her. Summer time found him in the small back garden attending his little flower patch; mending the shoes, painting the doors of the coal shed and the loo. To the outside world their life was very humdrum, but to them it was good. They had each other, their cat and dog, and not long ago Tom had brought her a Norfolk canary and a chaffinch.

To get back to all this would be heaven once again. Ruth hoped Tom had coped; it had been so very kind of him not to make a fuss when she had decided to come to Emma. She hoped she would never have to leave him again. So it was now arranged that Henry, who had been sent over to the flat to pack Diane's belongings, should escort Ruth back to London.

The wing in which Emma's room was situated in the hospital was very quiet on the afternoon that Ruth came to say goodbye. Emma was propped up, looking very pale and tired. Her eyes lit up with pleasure as she held a hand out to grasp one of Ruth's.

"Oh, Ruth dear, what should I have done without you? Nurse tells me today you have to go home. I feel sad you're going, but I hope you'll have me with you when I get away from here."

"Of course, Emma. You know you're always welcome; We love having you at any time. Lady Harkness tells me you're to be sent to the South of France to convalesce. She says it'll be very lovely there; she called the place Cannes, if I remember right. But

I'm sure you would have done just as well in Bournemouth or Brighton, and then me and Tom could have come to see you. This is not the time, really, to say all I think about you what you've gone through, and why, but when you're better don't be so ambitious, Em. Get home to the East End and settle down to some job or other in a factory. You'll meet some nice fella, like I met Tom, and then marry."

Walking towards the window, and keeping her back to Emma so the glistening tears which were ready to trickle down her face would not be seen, she continued, "I know people all over the world do the kind of things this young girl and young man did. I'm not able to find the right kind of words to use, and the last thing I want to do is to upset you. But you'll understand me when I say, try to keep away from these goings-on. I know we've been brought up a bit rough, and if I'd stayed at home maybe you wouldn't have wanted to get away so much. You would have grown up with me around. I loved you very much when you were a little nipper, and I don't think you would have wanted to leave me. But anyway, nothing can alter what's happened, but I feel you've had such a dreadful experience which you didn't deserve."

Ruth was almost breathless with so much talking; she was not given as a rule to outward expression, but she had thought it her loving duty to talk seriously to Emma. Turning back to the bed she wrapped Emma in her loving clasp. It never occurred to her that Emma should reply, and tell Ruth what she wanted.

"Be careful, now, Em," she said between raining kisses on her face, "don't get mixed up with these kind of people again. Directly you're well, come home to us. Be a good girl and write to us. All your belongings are at the hospital, so you won't need to return to that place again."

Straightening herself up and smoothing down her coat, Ruth then set her hat right. A tap at the door, and a young nurse beckoned that a cab and Henry were waiting. Just before she closed the door, Ruth looked back and said, "Say ta, ta, Em. Give us a smile to take back."

Emma, too full of grief for more than, "Bye for now" and a watery smile, turned her face as the door closed, and the tears flowed freely; not for Diane, not for Ruth, but for herself in her complete awareness of desolate loneliness in a strange country.

A week later Emma was transported in a hired car to recuperate in Cannes. She was still too weary to ask questions, and accepted the fact that Henry was always at hand. It seemed he had made all the arrangements for her departure, and he was now accompanying her. As the car left the hospital drive Henry said:

"It's a long journey and Lady Harkness has suggested that we break the journey and stay for the night in some hotel that'll be near at hand when you decide that you've had enough for one day. She thought a private car would be much better than train, with all the stops, and the disturbance of passengers getting in and out."

Putting his hand into his jacket pocket and then remembering he was with an invalid, Henry hastily withdrew it. Emma, noting the movement, gave a little whimsical smile and said, "You may smoke, Henry. It won't disturb me."

"Are you sure? Thanks", and within seconds he was drawing on a cigarette.

He felt nervous with Emma. She was not like the girl he used to know; the girl who would say so much with her eyes, yet who gave him a resounding smack if he took liberties. Well, of course, she had been very ill, and it would take time to recover from that awful shock. He would find it difficult to talk to her on the journey, he felt sure. She seemed so far away. He would tell her about the arrangements for her convalescence.

"Lady Harkness has been very anxious about you, and so she should. His Lordship has a small house in Cannes, which he often lets his friends use. At the moment it's vacant, and so they both thought they'd take up residence there and have you with them. The house is situated in the old town near Mount Chevalier. They both need to be away from England at this time. They're very badly shocked and upset. In fact, they look extremely ill. They temporarily engage French staff when they're in Cannes, but thought I might also come to be at hand and help you. I know you won't feel much like moving around, but at least you'll have an Englishman on hand. I know a bit of the country around Cannes, because a couple of friends and myself got a job there one season waiting for ships. We might be able to bathe, and take some walks when I'm off duty. This is, of course, when you're better."

Henry glanced at Emma, who lay back against the car, eyes closed. He thought she might be asleep, but her eyes opened. She smiled and said, "Thank you, Henry. I can't thank you enough for all you've done. I've felt very listless, and not inclined to talk, but I'm aware of all the trouble you've been put to. I know how you've been back and forward to England with my sister, and how considerate you were to her, and then all the trouble you've taken over me. All this was not of my making, and I know our employers told you what they wanted you to do. But you've done it all with such good grace, and shown me so much kindness, that I shall never be able to repay you."

"It's all right, old girl. Don't mention it any more. I jumped at the chance to be near you. I've been a bit of a rake but, if you remember, I did tell you once that I was falling in love with you. This is not the time to talk about it, but I really have fallen. Hurry and get well, so that you can pick me up. Say goodbye to Paris and all that horror, and look forward to brighter days."

"I will try, Henry," she whispered, "I will try." She closed her eyes and the agony in her heart was unbearable. "Goodbye," it said, "goodbye, Andrew. Goodbye Paris, city of enchantment."

Chapter Five

The Harknesses were already installed in their villa when Emma arrived. She felt very nervous at meeting them, and they were apparently equally so. Henry had taken her luggage to a room assigned to her, and Emma was seated in the sitting-room facing Lady Harkness while his Lordship stood looking out of the window into a small garden.

"Well, Emma, we hope you're feeling much better, and in the month you're with us you'll be fully restored to health. The beautiful sea air and sunshine will bring the colour back to your cheeks and you'll be fit again." Lady Harkness cleared her throat, fidgeted a little and, not looking at Emma continued, "We shall arrange for you to return to England, and shall give you references for another position."

Gosh! thought Emma, I'm being sacked. She's talking to me as though nothing dreadful has happened. Your daughter is dead! she wanted to scream. Murdered! Have you nothing to say to me about <u>her</u>? But, no, you wouldn't. I'm just a servant.

" - and so we thought." His Lordship had been speaking. Emma looked at him. He was turning towards her and she noticed how dreadfully ill he looked, "we thought that if we gave you this money, when you went back you would avoid talking to journalists who, no doubt, would find you and offer an equal sum of money for your story. There are always sensationalists who'll print and even serialise the misfortunes of others."

"Please, I don't understand what you're telling me. All I know is that I've experienced a dreadful tragedy, and been ill because of it. And now I want to get well and back to work. I shall never forget it, neither shall I ever forget Miss Diane." She saw Lady Harkness flinch at the mention of her daughter's name. "She was so very, very kind to me. Don't think, however, that I would wish to talk to anyone about it." Then, indignation rising within her, she continued, "I may not have education, or have the opportunities of other girls and boys, but at least I have a sense of honour and loyalty, and I would never wish to make anything out of this."

She could say no more because tears were already in her eyes, and her throat felt tight with emotion. She looked at both of them. How calm they seemed, confronted with so deep and intimate a tragedy. These kind of people were not like those of the East End. At home there would be much crying and talking, neighbours always running in to see if they could help, women for days gossiping over the backyard fence, and standing in little groups on their way to and from shopping. But these two were absolutely regal. The calmness of their features would never betray that their hearts were torn in the agony of their loss. They were stately, but beneath it all Emma knew their hearts must be breaking. What could she do to help them? Nothing, because not even to each other would they open their hearts. They would appear always calm, composed, the perfect lady and gentleman of breeding and inheritance. They would suffer much more than the people from whom Emma sprung; the working class had a way of talking of such things and so eventually exorcising their grief, getting it out of their system. Privations and social suffering had taught them, through the ages, to face each and every trouble stolidly. By so doing they had learned to live with it. Humour eventually came to their aid, and they would end up philosophically exclaiming, "There are worse troubles in the sea!" or, "You can always see worse around you if you stop to look!" or maybe, "God knows best, and this is life, and no crying will alter it."

Emma warmed towards these two, who would never enjoy the rough humour of her background.

"We have Henry here to do small duties, and we thought you could help too by arranging flowers and other little things which will help you to feel useful. But our whole intention is that you should get out into the sunshine as much as possible and get well. We thought a month would be very good for you. During that time you can decide what you would like to do for future employment, as it would be most painful to you if you returned to our household in London. (And for you both too, Emma thought). We shall help and advise you to get a suitable position. With Henry here, you'll take your meals in the staff room, and not be embarrassed with the remainder of the staff. They're local people who know nothing of the recent events. (Emma again thought, You don't know how quickly rumour flies, and I guess they already know, even if their facts are a bit shaky.) So naturally we shall expect that neither you nor Henry will discuss them." Lady Harkness looked towards his Lordship, who took up the conversation.

"My solicitor is here on holiday, and he will be seeing you in a day or two. I've decided that in lieu, as it were, of notice to leave us, at the end of your stay here I shall give you two hundred pounds, plus your monthly salary for the next year. You will realise that we do not know much about you, and this money is to be paid to you in case the temptation assails you to sell a sordid story. Now please listen!" Lady Hawkness said, as Emma rose to her feet and was about to interrupt. "It is because of your employment with us that you have suffered this dreadful ordeal," his Lordship cleared his throat and Emma realised that Diane's name would not cross his lips again. Whether he was ashamed, or just proud, she never knew. "But we do not know you well; we did not have you sufficiently long enough under our roof, but we feel that, having been chosen to go to Paris, you are trustworthy. We shall ask you to sign a document to the effect that you know why you are receiving the money. I hope you are clear on this point. And now, my dear," turning towards his wife, "I believe this matter is understood by Emma, and I am going into the garden."

Left alone with her Ladyship, Emma felt speechless and bewildered, and in a vague way she heard her say, "After lunch you must rest. The local doctor will call to see you, and will attend you each week while you are here." Rising, she rang a bell and Henry, who had been hovering outside, entered. "Tell one of the maids to show Emma her room." Turning to Emma, she said "it is small because you will not have to share it. I thought this best all round." And so within a very short time Emma was in her room unpacking. She felt nothing; she was all at sea. She must talk to Henry. Oh, that Ruth were here!

It was after the evening meal that Henry took Emma for a walk towards the harbour. It was filled with yachts, mainly belonging to rich foreigners. They were all lit up, brilliant and gay, and dimmed the stars in the beautiful Riviera sky.

"What a beautiful sight, Henry, just like fairyland!" exclaimed Emma. "It must be wonderful to be rich and enjoy all these luxuries. Tell me, did Diane come here often, and did she have many young friends with her here?

"Well, Emma, I can't tell you too much about her because as you know, I haven't been with the family very long, but she was always a young lady who enjoyed life and who would gather her friends around her wherever she went. I imagine she came here with her parents and had a whale of a time. I must show you around while you're here. We must watch a sunset together over the Estoril, and walk up the boulevards of La Californie.

Then there are the woods of La Maure; the French maid back at the house told me about them. She said there are trees of eucalyptus, mimosa, pines and heather there. We might also go to Saint Honorat, where there's a monastery. I understand it was built in the fifth century."

"Shall I have time for all these things? A month passes very quickly. You seem to know quite a lot about this place. Where did you get the knowledge - surely not all from the French maid in the few hours we've been here?"

"Oh, no!" Henry said rather sheepishly, "When I knew I'd be coming here, I bought a guide book. I thought if I'm to be your escort, I should know a little of the surrounding country, so I could interest you. No good the blind leading the blind, Em." And he gave her arm an affectionate squeeze.

A smile hovered over Emma's lips. How kind he is, she thought, gentle too; not a bit like the old Henry of Belgravia. He made her feel safe, and not so much alone.

"I want to tell you what they said to me today when I first arrived. It seems I'm to be here for one month, and then I must return home to find fresh employment. I am to go to a solicitor to sign an agreement that I won't let any member of the press interview me about Diane's death. In return I'll receive two hundred pounds and a monthly salary for a year. I feel dreadful to think they want to buy me off, and I've decided to refuse it."

"Nonsense, old girl. This affair was none of your making. I'm very matter of fact. Take what's offered you. Remember that Diane might have been kind and friendly with you, but she used you, you know. I'll always believe that your company was mostly needed as a blind."

"Henry, I don't believe it! She's dead! She was kindness itself to me. I shall never forget her. Don't discuss her with me any more, but leave me with the thought that she really liked me, and wanted me to be her companion, and had no other motive."

"All right, all right, old thing," Henry said with a soothing inflexion in his voice, "I'll leave you to your dreams. But <u>do</u> be advised on one thing - take the money offered you. You're poor, and it may be a little time before you get another job. The monthly salary won't keep you while you're looking round, because when you're in service you receive your keep too, remember. They really owe it to you, and as a matter of fact I don't think it's enough."

"You sound very logical, Henry. Put that way, I'll think it over. I have very little money, because I often paid for taxis and small items which were settled at the end of each month. There was quite a bit owed to me."

"Ask for it, Emma. You're regarded as a servant. Act like one." But she made no reply.

They made their way back. The night was still young, but Emma tired quickly. She thought she would like a bath and then go to bed, but the moment she thought of bed alone in a room, she was stricken with inward terror. In the hospital she had always seen a nurse when she woke in the night. On the journey down she had taken a sleeping draught that had been given to her, and she had slept dreamlessly throughout the night. In Paris, the change of atmosphere, with so many things to do,so <u>much</u> to do, had meant that she had gone to bed excited, eager to get to sleep so she could awaken to another day. On the odd occasion when she had been terrified, she had used her childhood cunning and gone into Diane's room saying, "Did you call?" or "I've had an unpleasant dream." And Diane, who seemed never to sleep for long, would reply, "Get your bed cover and lie on the sofa and talk for a while, and you'll soon calm down."

She seemed to understand. But now Diane had gone, and had left behind the horror of her death, to be added to all the other terrors that haunted Emma by night. "I think I should go to bed, Henry; and you must be tired too."

"I am rather, but before I go I have one or two jobs to do. The breakfast table to lay, and the shoes to clean. Leave yours out too, Emma. On my way up, I'll look in with some warm milk and a biscuit. Put a little whisky in it - do you no end of good!"

"No whisky, thank you, but the milk will be welcome." Emma was grasping any little attention now to prolong the time when she would be alone. "Oh, God!" she thought, as she ascended the stairs, "Help me, don't let me be frightened!" She tried to hum to herself as she prepared for bed. Her room was quite small, and so the side table light did not cast shadows into the corners. There was no verandah, for which she was thankful; that was one terror out of the way. She looked into the wardrobe cupboard - not big enough for anyone to hide in; under the bed - no one there. And then suddenly she was very angry with herself for deliberately frightening herself. She knelt down to say a prayer. Nothing seemed to come, and all she could say was, "God, you know what is in my heart and in my mind. Please help me, and keep me safe. Amen."

Rising, she turned the key in the lock, but immediately turned it back, for she remembered Henry was bringing her milk. She got into bed, a beautiful soft bed with huge pillows, and thought, "How tired I am. I'll go to sleep directly Henry brings my milk."

A gentle tap, and Henry was in the room, saying, "Here you are, Emma." Then he stopped as he placed the tray on the bedside table. He caught his breath. She looked lovely lying against the propped pillows, her beautiful black hair in one thick plait over a shoulder, her beautiful eyes, heavily lidded with the dark shadows of her recent illness, watching him. Her arms lay on either side of her. He wanted so much to touch her shoulders which were almost bare, and the gentle rise and fall of her bosom tempted him.

"Oh, thank you, Henry, you're always so kind to me. I hope I shall soon be asleep. Is there something wrong?" As he still stood and looked down on her.

"No, of course not. I just can't help looking at you, Emma, you're lovely, and I love you."

He put out a hand and touched her arm. She withdrew it, and said, "Nonsense, Henry. You tell all the girls that. You must go, Henry. I can hear footsteps somewhere." A door banged on another floor.

"Oh, that must be the other staff going. There's only the cook and myself that sleep in. The Harknesses have their room on the floor below; the cook on the kitchen floor. I have a room at the end of this corridor. The other two rooms on this floor are the guest room and the bathroom. So if you need anything, I'm close at hand." He bent and kissed her gently on the cheek and then, looking into her eyes, gathered her up and kissed her mouth.

Drawing back, she said, "Good night, Henry. see you in the morning", and when he had closed the door she got out and turned the key. Very shortly afterwards she turned out the light and gradually drifted into sleep. The booming of a clock woke her. All was dark; all was quiet, and dreamily she turned over to sleep again, when suddenly she became wide, wide, startingly wide awake. Immediately terror beset her. She began to tremble, her eyes wide open. "Oh, please, please, God, keep me safe!" she prayed. She turned over. Was there something beside her. She turned on the light; should she keep it on? Would some unseen Thing switch it off? She would switch it off herself first. She lay on her back; would the ceiling come down on her? Had she looked well into the wardrobe? Had something crept into the room and under the bed when Henry opened the door? Was that a movement outside? She was trembling like a leaf; everywhere was hushed. She saw a light in the corner of her room. What was it? It had gone. Stupid! It must have been the light of a passing vehicle. She must get her head well under the clothes, and try to go to sleep. That was better, she couldn't see anything. But no, something might press the clothes tight against her head. Uncover quickly - and keep your eyes open! Now I can see. I can pick out the furniture, and the window. Did I lock the window? Shall I see something pressing against the panes? I'll put the light on again. The trembling hand knocked over the lamp instead. She began to cry. I'm not safe. What shall I do? Henry, yes, Henry. The thought was there. I must go to him. He'll save me. She was out of bed, out into the dark corridor, and along to Henry's room.

She stood against the door, her face pressed into it as though for protection; her hand sought the door knob, and she gently turned it. The door opened and then, within a second, she was inside and had closed the door. The room was dark, and she couldn't see, but the sound of gentle breathing reached her fuddled brain.

"Henry, Henry!" she whispered tremulously, and then she moved towards the sound of his breathing. One of her knees touched the side of his bed, and at the same time she bent to touch him. He sprang, caught her arm, and at the same time, she said, "Oh, I'm so frightened!" and he, "What on earth's the matter, Emma?" He was awake in a second. He had been startled by what he thought was an intruder. And more than ever startled when she got in beside him, clinging and crying, "Henry, help me! I'm frightened. Am I safe?" and when he tried to get a little away from her, she held tighter, trembling, and he, experienced with women as he was, tried to unlace her fingers that seemed to clasp his neck so firmly to her.

"Emma! Emma!" he mumbled somewhere into her hair. He could not get away. "Tell me, what's the matter? Let go and tell me." But she still went on, mumbling and crying, and shaking with fear. He wedged his hands between their bodies, gave a sharp wrench and he was free.

Springing out towards the switch, the room was soon alight, and he gazed down at her, startled to see the hair around her head in wild disorder, her white, tear-stained face, and her eyes so pathetic. Her sobs were quieter now, as he lit a cigarette, but his thoughts tumbled one over the other. He had plenty of experience with women; he was made that way. "Love `em and leave `em" had always been his motto. But Emma had always been a different proposition. At first he had tried the usual tactics, and had been rejected. She had got under his skin as no other had done, and with all the trouble she had experienced, he had been at hand to give her some help; and now he began to realise he was coming to love her, and the desire to marry her was taking hold of him.

He sat in a chair smoking, watching her, trying to form words that would dissolve his uncertainty as to why she had come to him. Was it an act? Was this another way of saying "Yes, you can have me?" Women were so wily in their ways. Was she a little mad from her dreadful ordeal, and if so, shouldn't she be in hospital under treatment? He watched as his cigarette burned to an end. She had drawn the covers up to her chin, and her eyes were closed. Crushing the end out, Henry walked to the bed and said in a very low voice,

"Look here, Emma, I don't know what to do about all this. You must have had a bad dream, and in a little while you'll be fine. I'll take you back to your room. Shall I get a drink for you?" he asked, reaching for his gown.

In a flash, she sat up and caught his hand. "Don't go, Henry. Don't leave me! I feel safe if you're here." And he, looking down at her, not understanding fear, the stark, raving fear of what she had experienced, thought that only a bad dream had upset her, and now this was an invitation.

He turned off the light and got into bed, gathering her into his arms.

The warmth and comfort of him gave peace to her tortured mind. She was safe. She drifted into false security. With love words and gentle hands he took her, and in the passion that swept her she gave, and gave again when pain had left her, and finally they slept in each other's arms.

Chapter Six

To try to explain to Henry in broad daylight the fears that beset her at night was impossible, and in any case, even to her they were not at all real and receded with the coming day. As for Henry, he just looked back and was grateful for the nightmare. Their employers did not interfere with any of the ample leisure they were both given, and by the end of two weeks of lazing in the sunshine and taking meals at night in a little café they had found, it had become an expected arrangement that they should sleep together. Sometimes she would repel him and he would have to be content that she was in his bed, close to him. Sometimes she was, if it were possible, more passionate and demanding than he. But he loved her very much, and day by day his love deepened. He wanted very much to marry her, and sometimes after their lovemaking, full of contentment, he would broach the subject; but she, equally content, would murmur sleepily, "Let's talk tomorrow, dear." But tomorrow never seemed to come.

With this always happening, Henry decided, as they sat drinking coffee in the little café, to ask, "When will we get married, darling? I can quite easily get a job in a hotel or restaurant when we return to London, and I'll come home every night. I've got enough money to get a little house and make a good home for us both."

"But I don't want to marry. I want to be free for ages. I don't feel as though I want your little house with its monotony of everyday cleaning, washing, shopping."

But there'll be babies to care for. They take up lots of time, so you'll be a very busy little mother."

"That's just it. I don't want to be a very busy little mother." Pushing the pram up the High Street, talking and admiring other people's babies on the way, exchanging little tit-bits of news, sitting in baby clinics, listening to advice, worrying over teething troubles, baby rash, and baby ailments. I'm not old enough myself. I want to be free."

"But how can you be free after all this love-making? You love me, you tell me so, and lightly not either, when we're together."

"Henry, you're older than I am in years, but at this moment I feel older than you, and wiser. I'm not by any means the first girl you've had, and you must realise that what I am saying in bed are just words of love I utter during sex. I'm very fond of you, but inexperienced as I was until I came to your bed, I know that during sex the emotions are stretched to breaking point. I get more satisfaction from our love-making when I use the words I do. When I'm in your arms, and you're in mine, I say, 'I love you.' because I know when you hear it, I excite you more. At that time I do love you. I love what you give me, I love the rhythm of our bodies, it's ecstasy to me, and I would willingly die before it all ends. But looking at you in the clear light of day, I know I don't love you in the complete sense. I know I couldn't, for the rest of my life, cook for you, drudge around the house for you, and rear your squawling babies."

He looked across at her, speechless. Was this the girl whose arms encircled him, whose lips whispered into his ear the love words that so delighted him? He knew that a fortnight earlier she had been a virgin. She'd been ignorant then - or had she? She had given herself as an experienced woman would. She'd enjoyed every moment of it. She was demanding, exhausting at times, and he had believed she was in love with him. He looked hard at her; she looked so young, beautiful and innocent. Who would have believed it? He felt bitter, frustrated, humiliated. He felt raped. A born whore, that's what you are, you bitch, a born whore! he thought. And then aloud, trying to keep emotion out of his voice, he said, "I suppose this is the end, Emma? Have you finished with my love-making?"

Toying with an empty match box that lay in an ash-tray, Emma avoided looking at him. Thoughts crowded her mind. She could not tell him that at first she had paid a price for her fear, but had then come to like his love-making. During it she had washed away the terrors that beset her, or at least they lay dormant. During the day his bright friendliness helped her to forget the recent tragedy. She had had very little affection in her life, and with him she had found some. She could not deny to herself that she liked it, and during the day looked forward to the night with him. Perhaps, when she tired of him, she would be able to forget it all - or would she? If not, what then? Looking up she said, "Drink up your coffee, Henry, and don't look at me so fiercely. Congratulate yourself that you're not saddled with a wife, but that you have a lover instead. It's more exciting!"

"You flabbergast me, Emma! Do you mean that we're to carry on just the same?" And inwardly he thought, Harlot, whore. I could kill you. I thought only men carried on this way. Yet I can't resist you. I love you, I'll do anything to keep you. Bitch! Vampire! Emptying the coffee hastily down his throat, he rose and they left hand in hand.

Emma had met the solicitor and discussed the terms under which she should receive the money Lord Harkness had offered her. She had listened to Henry and, without any qualms, signed the agreement required. She was now the possessor of a fair sum of money, added to which was not the monthly salary she had received when she first became a servant, but the twenty pounds a month Diane had given her as her companion in Paris, and this for the following tweve months! To say she was astonished was putting it rather mildly, but she decided not to tell Henry about it. She sat in her room and added up her resources. Two hundred pounds twenty pounds a month. She would be a fool to marry. She could still see a little of the world. There would be time enough to settle. She liked Henry well enough, but Paris had spoilt her. How she would eventually get free of him she had not yet devised - that would resolve itself, she felt sure.

In the meantime there was still another week to be enjoyed in Cannes. Today she would go out alone. She enjoyed the beach, and would go to Antibes, its golden sand stretching for more than three miles. She took a cab to the Golfe-Juan, and viewed the memorial which commemorated Napoleon's last venture from the Isle of Elba, when he landed on the 'Inconstante' with thousands of men. It had been a deserted spot in those days, and perhaps still was in winter; but now the beach was crowded with bathers.Walking towards Juan Les Pins Emma noticed the many tourists, and knew by their accents, that they were mostly American. The Casino gardens were beautiful, and she seated herself near the triumphant monument. She did not know what it stood for, but knew history was here. She closed her eyes. With this money she could go from place to place, and enjoy life. There was so much in this world. She wanted to know and see a little of it. But could she do it alone? What could she do about the terrors that beset her at night? Who could help her? No one, just herself. Added to it was thc horror of Diane's death; in spite of her efforts it haunted her at odd moments, when she seemed to be forgetting it. Her new inheritance reminded her of it all the more, and all she could now think of was Diane and John; Diane mostly, amongst those flowers, smiling at her. And she felt so alone. She must try to fight this terror. It had been getting so much better with Diane.

The sun was pouring down upon her upturned face, her eyes still closed, dreaming away. Yes, dreaming away - or, was she dreaming, for a voice from the recent past was saying, "Dreaming again?" She knew that voice! Could it be true? Open your eyes! No! let me dream. But a real warm live hand took one of hers, and involuntarily she looked into the blue eyes of Andrew Craig!

As she jumped to her feet, startled and bewildered, he was saying, "I couldn't believe my eyes, finding you again, dreaming away as you were the day in the Louvre when we first met." Trying to compose herself Emma greeted him, and tried to answer his questions.

He had heard about the tragedy and had tried to see her in hospital, but had been told that visitors were not allowed. A woman had spoken to him in a little waiting room when he'd come to make enquiries; he'd thought she was some relative because she had spoken of taking Emma home when she was fit to travel. She had been rather short with him, and told him that Emma would not have been in this trouble if she had not been so eager to leave home amd mix with her so called 'betters'. The next time he had called he'd learned where Emma had gone and decided that as soon as possible he would travel to Florence. He'd been in Antibes for a week and intended to visit Cannes the following day. All this he told her, none of it penetrating Emma's excited brain; all she could think of was that he was here, that it was all wonderful.

They went first, as she had intended, to Antibes and had tea in his hotel. They seemed so happy in each other's presence. He suggested they walk to the church, for there was a most beautiful picture he would like to show her. It was named 'The Virgin of the Rosary'. Emma was awed by its magnificence, while Andrew explained its measurements and mysteries.

"It's approximately fifteen feet high by thirteen wide," he said. "You'll see the Virgin is carrying the Baby Jesus and holds the Rosary in her hand. Those around her praying are priests and great lords. It's supposed to have been painted by Francios Bre'a around 1515."

"You know so much about art," said Emma, "I wish I did. I'd love to travel from place to place."

"Then you must come to Florence with me," Andrew replied with a flippant laugh, "you'll find plenty there to discover." And squeezing her arm, he said "Why not, Emma, why not come with me?"

A breathless silence; she trembled at the thought. Who would stop her? no one! Emma glanced up and saw Andrew's smiling quizzical look, and silently echoed his question, "Why not?"

Aloud she returned, "Do you really mean it? Shall I come with you? What shall I do? I have a little money to pay my fare. I could come whenever you say."

"Easy, easy. I was in a way, joking, but I feel more serious now. Let's have an apéritif and then dine together."

The evening passed quickly in each other's company. Andrew was on his way to Florence, he told her, to see some friends, perhaps, and enjoy the art galleries. His father expected him eventually to go into the family business, but until pressure was put on him, he felt he would like to roam around Europe and enjoy himself. His private income would more than take care of his needs. Looking at Emma across the table, he felt again the fascination creep over him that he had experienced with her that night in Paris.

She's a charmer, he thought; perhaps not out of the top drawer, at least that's what his parents and friends would say. But then, of course, they would never meet her, and in the meantime, here she was, ready for the plucking, and he had only to stretch out his hand. She would be a delightful companion to take with him, and in the artistic circles in which he moved, no one would raise an eyebrow.. So, looking still further into her lovely eyes to try to read her real thoughts, he asked: "Were you serious about joining me in Florence?" and was taken aback by the forthright question. Which was her reply.

"Tell me," she said raising her eyebrows and involuntarily clasping her hands together, "tell me, what exactly is in your mind with regard to me?"

It was Andrew who lowered his eyes for a few moments, colour suffusing his cheeks. "Well," he responded with a nervous laugh, "this is, of course, all very sudden, and natually what at first was a joke has now become a serious invitation, so I'll now repeat it. Emma, why not come with me to Florence, because may I add, I wish it very much?"

And being very outspoken, she did not hesitate to enquire, "As your maid, your friend, or your mistress?"

"Emma! How outspoken you are for one so young! You quite startle me!" There was silence for a second or so as he reached for her hand, and looking at her, so appealing, so different from the girls he was accustomed to, he was conscious of the thoughts he had had about her a little earlier, and conscious also of a little flutter in his heart, which should have warned him that he might fall in love with her.

"Shall we say we'll travel to Florence together as friends, like old family friends, and let fate decide the rest?"

"Well, yes, that's fair enough. It'll be wonderful to go with you. It will solve the problem of what Lady Harkness wishes to do with me. Oh, don't look alarmed!" she added as a lightning look of alarm fluttered across his face. I won't tell her anything. I shall only say that I'll be leaving on the day you tell me. I've been given two hundred pounds in lieu of notice, and a year's salary. I shall not be quite penniless, and I have forty pounds saved!"

Andrew threw his head back and gave a hearty laugh. "Oh, Emma, what a fortune you have!" and then quite soberly he added, "Take care of it for some future purpose. I shall take care of all your expenses. I extended the invitation. Already I'm eager for us to be gone. The prospect of your company excites me; I hope you'll feel the same."

"I shall. I mean, I do already, and I'm very grateful. And now, will you find me a cab? Will you phone me to tell me when to go?"

"I believe I can settle it now. Let me see, this is Friday. Could you be ready on Monday? Send most of your luggage to my hotel, I'll attend to it. And now, goodbye until then. By the way, if you change your mind, don't hesitate to tell me. I'll try to understand."

He took her swiftly into his arms as she about to get into the cab, and gave her a warm, deep kiss. Then, standing a little back from her, he said, "A kiss, my Emma, to seal our plans."

Lying back in the cab, eyes alight, lips parted in eager anticipation, Emma was almost back in Cannes before she realised there was still Henry to deal with. She had to break the news of her going, but definitely not with whom she was going, and where.

That night, in the darkness of his room, with his arms around her, she told him. There was a breathless silence about him; everything was so still for a while Emma was frightened. She broke it by saying, "Say something, Henry. I'm not committing a crime. I can't stay here forever."

"I know, but where are you going? Tell me. If you must go, let me come with you. I won't press you to marry me until you say so. I won't ever mention it again, but don't leave me!" he cried drawing her tighter into his arms.

"No, Henry. I'm going away. I want to be alone, and I've made no plans." She pushed him away as she said it and he, cried from the fear of losing her, loving her as he did, in his anguish called her aloud a whore, a harlot. Fiercely his passions swept him, and she was defenceless in his embrace. Then she too was consumed in the fierceness of his love-making; they climbed the furthest mountain top together, returned exhausted, spent, a fathomless abyss, and in his hunger and despair, ere the night departed, he gave her the child of his lust.

Remorse entered into her soul, and for the next two days and nights she did not go anywhere near Henry. Fate took a hand in settling everything for her departure, for early on the Monday she discovered that Henry was taking the Harknesses by car to Antibes.

She kept to her room until they had gone, and with all her packing completed, called a cab. It was not until she had left the house that she gave her destination to the driver.

Andrew was waiting in the lobby hoping, he said, for a phone call, but here she was, a thousand times better; and with his own luggage all ready for the station waggon, he settled his account and they departed.

Milan was the first port of call. They stayed two days. She was so excited that she had no time for fear. In Bologna, where they remained a week, she was so tired that she went into a dreamless, fearless sleep each night. And now they had arrived in Florence, and checked into the San Lorenzo Hotel.

"I hope you'll find your room comfortable," said Andrew as they entered the lift. "I suggested one next to mine, which has a perfect view of the Ponte Vecchio."

At dinner that night Emma was very excited. She was fascinated by the splendour of the dinning-room, the waiters in their white monkey jackets moving noiselessly around the tables. Andrew ordered with authority and knowledge. He treated her with such perfect consideration, especially over the wines, and tactfully said in the hearing of the waiter, "I'll choose for us both, my dear." Her eyes were luminous in the light of the table lamp; her beautiful dark hair had, or so it seemed to him, a very special glow, and somehow in its midst a blue ribbon was entwined and came to rest in the coil of her hair at the nape of her neck. Her mouth was full and shining with scarlet lipstick, the lower lip slightly thrust forward, and the faintest glimpse of her upper teeth, white and beautiful, attracted his gaze, held him, and he felt the blood bounding in his temples.

With great effort he said, "Have you lost your tongue?"

"Oh, no. I'm busy watching everything and everybody."

"You like it here, the hotel?"

"Why, yes, of course. Why do you ask? Have I given you reason to think otherwise? This is all very new, and I find it a bit difficult to make conversation. But," she said hastily, in order to assure him, "by tomorrow I'll be quite settled in."

He searched her eyes, her hand was quietly drawn into his, and he said, "Let's dispense with coffee. Get a wrap and we'll stroll along the Arno."

The autumn sun had slowly sunk, and the evening star beckoned. For a time they walked silently along the banks, leaving the city behind them. She looked up at him, wanting to say so much, her heart filled with gratitude to be here with him, everything and everyone forgotten; just now and for a while, at least, there was just Andrew and herself. A few more seconds passed before he threw his cigarette stub into the river and broke the silence.

"I've been thinking of when we first met, our evening out and how attracted I was to you. There's something very fascinating about you. I'm glad you came here with me, but I must be honest. When I first invited you, it was only in a very frivolous way. I had no idea that you would accept, neither had I any particular inclination for you to come. But directly you said you would, I began to look forward to it, and now I believe I'm falling in love with you."

A smile crept over her face as she listened. She was happy, so very, very happy; this was what she wanted; him to love her, to love her now, as she knew she loved him. Tomorrow could take care of itself; tomorrow never came; it was today, today always. She stopped and looked up at him; he drew her closer in the gathering dusk, kissed her with tenderness that swiftly turned to passion, and just as hastily he let her go.

"May I sleep with you tonight? Do you want me as I want you?"

"Yes, yes!" she cried, clasping the hand that rested on her shoulder, "I want you just as much as you want me. Let's go back to the hotel now, Andrew."

The orchestra was playing an English dance as they entered. "Let's dance for a while," he said, and she followed him. To the tune of 'I can't give you anything but love, baby,' they foxtrotted, he singing the chorus to her very quietly.

"That's what I shall call you," he said.

"Call me what?"

"Baby, of course, my love name for you. Baby when we're alone, Emma in public, when we have to be formal!"

He held her close, she smiling with parted lips until they came to the edge of the floor, and then he led her into the hall. She gathered her wrap while he collected their keys, and without a word entered the lift to their rooms. Lightly he kissed her, and opened her door, taking out the key and handing it to her.

"Lock your door, darling, I'll come across the balcony," he said, and entered his own room, whistling.

He crossed to the French window of her room which stood open so that the cool air stirred the net curtains which hung loosely to the floor. He watched her as he made her way to the dressing table, brushing her beautiful hair that hung thick by her waist, looking like a mantle over her nightgown which was almost transparent and clung in a magical way to her body. He shook his head wonderingly. How young she looked, and yet now full of wisdom - all she would ever need, and she had man sense, the sense that most women were always seeking and never found. She turned, put down her brush and came towards him; without a word he lifted her and put her on the bed. Discarding his robe he lay beside her, she as quiet as he. Then suddenly he was upon her, crushing her mouth with his seeking lips and tongue. Her arms held him and his hands were seeking, and then he entered her, and she gave herself with a passion equal to his own. Like two tired animls, they finally slept in each other's arms.

When Emma awoke next morning, she stirred lazily like a kitten and stretched a hand towards Andrew. She was startled into sudden wakefulness to find him gone. Her vision cleared and she saw him leaning on the balustrade of the balcony. How wonderful it was, she thought, and "Andrew, come here!" He turned and came to her, loving her, caressing her, and she returned his love.

"I love you, baby, I love you," he repeated over and over. She clung to him for fear of losing him, she gave as only one can give who loves, as she loved him, as she would love him forever; because in all the years that lay before her, and when he had gone from her forever, she did not know it now, but this was the hour that would be with her for always, and in her old age she would hear him as he repeated a few lines from that foolish song, "I can't give you anything but love, Baby."

Chapter Seven

The days passed lazily. Closer and closer they grew together so that not only were they in love with each other, but loved each other too. Several times Emma saw a quiet thoughtful look on Andrew's face, and often she felt he wanted to ask her a question, but for some reason he did not. It seemed as though neither had a care in the world, that the world had commenced only when they first became lovers. If he ever gave a thought to the past she was not aware of it, but her love for him grew and grew; it was so absorbing that never for a fleeting moment did Henry, Diane, Ruth or her mother ever creep out from the dim corners of her subconscious. Where they would eventually travel, what they would do, she never thought. To wake each morning in his arms, to love, to be loved, sometimes with passion, but always with the sincerity of his love in evidence, was more then enough for Emma. In the quietness of the night, she would sometimes wake and lie with pleasure in the warmth of his body, and she marvelled as she lay there that he loved her so much. He was kind, gentle and considerate. She was maturing and love had made her even more beautiful; her eyes were always shining; she would sing, and her happy laughter would ring out over the roof tops of the brown and gold buildings of Florence; echo into the heavens and return. He bought her lovely clothes, saucy hats that perched in a provocative manner on her hair. He gave her a beautiful ring, a topaz encircled with diamonds. He said, "Topaz, Baby, because you were born in November." They went on daily outings, the Duomo, Uffizi Gallery, the Pitti Palace, famous churches, museums. She absorbed it all, loving Florence for its beauty and culture, and the mystical air that embraced it. She stood with Andrew on the spot where legend says Dante first saw his Beatrice, and he said, "Not like us, darling. We've met and are together, but its said that Dante never spoke to his Beatrice, yet he had fallen in love with her on the spot and continued to love her for the rest of his life."

"I can't understand that. Why ever couldn't they meet again and he get to know her?"

"Well, let's not go into all that now. I'm thirsty. Let's have a drink."

Laughingly they settled for a café quite near the Arno and drank some wine. "After lunch I'm taking you to a beautiful spot above Florence, where there's a little villa I think you'll like. Fiesole is the name of the village. The villas are very beautiful; most of them behind high walls, with beautiful gardens. If this villa's to your liking, I shall take it for a while, and we can set up house together.

"Andrew! A house for both of us to live in? Forever?" Jumping up, she cried, "Quickly, darling, let's have lunch and go."

He laughed light-heartedly at her excitement, and the childish pleasure which crossed her face, and with no more ado he followed her.

The villa stood at the top of a narrow winding road climbing into the heights of Fiesole. A high brown wall surrounded it, with a large heavy door opening into a courtyard, at the side of which grew some olive trees. Crossing the courtyard Andrew pulled a bell. The door swung open noiselessly and a middle-aged serving woman smiled a greeting.

"Buon giorno, signori," she said, making a little bobbing curtsey, and with a broad smile she opened the door widely as a welcome.

"We shall like to look over the villa - Maria - I believe you are called? You know my name from the agent. This," he said, bringing Emma before him, "this is Signorina Emma Greaves."

Maria Rossi, with wide experience of people who had come and gone from the Villa Violetta, quickly summed up the relationship between these two very enthusiastic people, who were rapidly falling in love with it. They viewed and admired the kitchen and the long living-room with its tall French windows that opened out on to a garden filled with ferns and crimson geraniums. At the farthest end of the garden was an arbour covered with climbing vines, and beneath a wrought iron table and chairs.

"We'll be able to take our meals here. It'll be such fun - look, Andrew, a ginger cat!" The cat had jumped on to the table and was busily washing its face. Turning to Maria Emma asked, "What do you call it?"

"Ah, signorina," she faltered, in very uncertain English, "it is much bad gatto, molti babino. Come, Anna, we shall take the milk. Scusi, signori, maybe yes, you will see upstairs insieme." And with another little curtsey Maria gathered the cat in her arms and made towards the kitchen.

It took very little time for both to decide that this should be their home, their love nest. Andrew had understood that Maria would attend to the house and the needs of its occupants. She agreed that it would be better if she attended to the market, and fully understood that the signorina did not know the Italian language but would nevertheless like to superintend the small household. Maria was quiet and wise, and her manner was as soft as a gentle breeze on a summer evening. She liked the new occupants of the villa, and enjoyed the knowledge that they were lovers; but she was very cautious that her employer should not realise this. She shut her eyes to the fact that only one bedroom was occupied, and that Emma and Andrew were poles apart in their social way of life. For instance, Maria noticed that everyday things the signori took for granted, while the girl was always expressing her delight at the most ordinary things. She watched quietly and made many mental observations - for instance, she noted that at times he was quiet and thoughtful. She noticed also that the girl was sometimes a little pale in the morning, refusing her coffee; and to Andrew's enquiry Emma would try to satisfy him by saying she preferred a cold drink at any time to coffee. But before Emma knew it herself, Maria knew that the young woman was with child.

When the frightening knowledge came to her, Emma panicked. What would Andrew say? He had always told her that nothing like this would ever happen. She had believed him, and trusted him, and so had not worried. It was nearly three months since they had been together, and it was now evident that she was going to have a baby. He found her one morning vomiting her heart out, and with a sudden shock it came to him.

"Emma, Baby. It can't be!"

She recovered, washed her face in cold water and buried it in a towel. From its depths she said, "I'm afraid it's true, dear, and I'm frightened; what will become of me?"

"Come into the bedroom and sit down, we can talk it over," he said, leading her gently to a chair. "Are you quite sure, it's not the Italian food that's upset you?"

"No. Of that I am sure.

"But," said Andrew, with a little furrow between his brows, "but, Emma, I could have sworn that you wouldn't have a child. Darling, what shall we do? Forgive me! I'm a bit excited and can't think. Of course, we'll love it, it's wonderful news, dear; we'll become very happy parents." And he gathered her into his arms and kissed her, murmuring, "Imagine, my Emma with a little baby, and she herself a baby!"

Drawing away, and looking deeply into his eyes, Emma could see that Andrew did not mean it. He was as scared as she. She was not prepared for motherhood, she did not want a baby; she only wanted to go on loving Andrew; to be with him, laughing and happy - no cares, no responsibilities, which a baby would bring. And then the startled fact occurred to her, that she was not married to him, that this knowledge was already bringing doubts and uncertainties. Never once had marriage entered into their conversation, and hardly ever into Emma's mind. She loved Andrew very deeply and, in her simplicity, thought he felt likewise. Even with a child on the way, she felt no worry about their relationship. All she could think of at that moment was that the child would divert her attention from him.

In Andrew's mind there had been a lurking suspicion, which in the heat of his passion for her, and hers for him, he had lulled into the subconsciousness. But now the doubt suddenly awoke, and emerged into the broad daylight of his active mind. He remembered how there had been no difficulty when they had first made love, and that a certain shyness, apparent in most virgins had seemed absent in Emma. Had she had a lover before him? He was so convinced he had seen to it that she would not become pregnant. Could it be...? But he hastily stifled his thoughts. The whole point was that she was going to have a baby; he loved her very much, although at the beginning it had been no more than a casual love affair. She had a way with her; she had wound herself around his heart; he loved her and loving her, he must accept what was now his responsibility.

"My darling, Baby!" he smiled, gathering her into his arms and stroking her hair, "my darling, it seems I'm to have two babies now. We must decide what to do, and what's best for you. We shall get married, but in England, and stay there until the baby is born. Then we can decide to come back if we want, and bring a nanny with us.

But all Emma, with a certain quietness, could only reply, "We can't make plans right away, darling. First I must ask Maria to take me to a doctor. When he has convinced me that we are to have a baby, then we can plan." Like all men, on points of this kind, Andrew gave in.

An English doctor was found; he seemed very understanding, asking as few questions as possible when he discovered Emma was unmarried. His verdict was like a death knell - she was much more than three months pregnant, and with that alarming knowledge came another blow. The child was Henry's not Andrew's!

Her mind was in turmoil. What could she do, what could she tell Andrew? Nothing. She would wait for a while; let him plan, and if this fitted in with all the other circumstances she would remain quiet. She loved him fiercely. To hell with Henry, curse him for doing this to her! She had no thought of what she had done to him, how she had used him, satisfied herself. Anyway, anything could happen; she might never carry the child that long. Now if she were at home at Stepney this could all be put right...And soon a plan began to form - Andrew said they would go to England and marry. She must encourage him to hasten the arrangements.

Rubbing her face against his collar, and kissing behind his ear as she sat in his lap that evening, she persuaded Andrew that it would be best to return as soon as possible. She intended to stay near her people, she said, until he got the special licence.

"What about your family? Will you tell them, and will they make a fuss?" Emma wanted to know.

"Yes, I'm certain of that, Baby. My mother has that strong conviction that no one is really good enough for her sons. My father - well, I can't say, because I suppose I realise he's always expected both my brother and I to make the kind of marriages, suitable to his position. So he's never discussed the possibility that we might do otherwise. I know when they meet you they'll soon learn to love you. But I do believe our best plan is to marry, return here, then let them know, hoping, of course, that they'll not meet us until after the child is born!"

Emma listened thoughtfully, but without comment. It would be wonderful to marry Andrew; then he really would be hers. Of the child - well, a baby didn't come into the pattern of her life; she wouldn't have it if she could help it. To get to England as soon as possible was uppermost in her mind, and then she would go to Ruth. Ruth would help. Their sort of people always helped each other; they would help her. Andrew need not even know. She could tell him her pregnancy had ended badly and he would think it had happened the natural way. He was a lamb, he would believe whatever she told him. Of course, there was the possibility that he might not marry her. But, of course, she knew he would, and that would prove more than ever that he loved her, and they would be happy.

Before they left for England, Emma recalled that the Harkness solicitors were responsible for her passage, so she quickly sent them a letter to forward the cost to Ruth's address.

As the cliffs of Dover came into sight, Andrew became very concerned with the arrangements she had made to stay with her own people while the wedding arrangements were being made.

"Why not stay somewhere in Kensington? It'll be much better, darling, and I can see you. Or better still, we can be at the same hotel."

"No, it's better this way," she demurred, "I can see my mother and sister; not, of course, to tell them anything about us, but to explain a little where I've been, and to tell them I'll be going away again soon. I can phone you, and you can tell me when and where I can meet you again."

"But don't you think to meet them, to lie and to be evasive, is not only unkind to them, but also untrue to our love, and the baby?"

He looked angry and somewhat bewildered. This was not his way. One did not go around making false statements; one should have the courage of one's own convictions. Glancing down at Emma he suddenly had the awful thought that she was using him, and that night, after she had taken the train for Liverpool Street, he checked into a hotel in Victoria and went straight to bed.

He could not sleep. He missed her, damn it, he was crazy with love for her, and he was tormented by his thoughts. Again he was assailed by thoughts of what she had been like before he knew her. Had she had another lover or, worse still, more than one? He thought of her in the arms of many, her beautiful white body and soft milk-like skin, beneath the gross, searching hands of some fat, lustful, lecherous bounder, whose coarseness demanded more than mere intercourse. This baby - had she known, when he had laughingly asked her to Florence? Had she been clever, and hoped to foster it upon him? Hr twisted and turned in his agony of mind, and the agony of his body that was in crying need for her. He flung himself out of bed, switched on the bedside lamp, lit a cigarette and gazed longingly at the telephone near at hand. If only he could speak to her, hear her voice - anything but this dreadful torment! Savagely he drew on his cigarette, trying to calm his thoughts, and conjure up the many living pictures of her and their brief time together, until at last he settled back into his lonely bed, and in the darkness drifted into sleep. In his dreams he saw his beloved, alive, tremulous, full of love and passion for him, offering herself to the assault of his love.

Chapter Eight

Ruth at first was very happy to have Emma back home again, but the news that she was 'in trouble' was not well received. If she had been courting an ordinary boy and this had happened, well, she would have been rushed to the altar right away, complete with white dress, orange blossom and all the trimmings. To go gallivanting all over the world, getting involved with murder, and mixing with people who were no better than those of the East End (in fact worse because they should know better) did not inspire in Ruth much sympathy for her sister.

Who's the father, and will he marry you?" She fumed. "No, he's had his pleasure," (never thinking that Emma had had hers too) "and no doubt, my girl, he'll even refuse to own it's his, let alone keep it. What will your mother say when she knows? Remember, you're still under age, and believe me, she'll have plenty to say. I know, she was a devil when I was a girl. She's forever carrying on about the way you left home for that London job, and then when she found out about your illness, and that I'd gone to Paris to see you, the world nearly blew up with her temper. She has it in for me because I didn't bring you home."

And so Ruth went on until she could find no more to say. She was surprised at herself saying so much, for she was by nature quiet. Having lived with Tom away from any family life, she found that Emma's troubles were becoming too frequent and each time worse. She had taken this opportunity to expound her theory about the man who had exposed Emma to this trouble, because they were both in the house alone; Tom had gone to an Union Meeting. Quite freely, Emma replied to all of this.

"As a matter of fact," she said, "I'm going to be married. But it's only you I can tell. Before I went away with Andrew - I think you met him in the hospital - I had an affair with someone else. I liked this person but never loved him, and I love Andrew. I haven't and can't tell him about Hen- well, about this other man. He believes the bab's his, and in a few days' time we're going to get married. But I want you to help me, introduce me to someone so that I can have an abortion -"

"A what!" said Ruth incredulously. "Do you mean to tell me that you want to get rid of it? Tell the other man you're going to have his kiddy, and he'll marry you. I noticed you tripped up and gave his name away. It's Henry, the footman, isn't it? Tell him, Emms, and tell this other chap the truth."

"I can't, and I won't!" cried Emma, stamping a foot, and then with a look of appeal: "Ruth, I love Andrew; he will marry me, but I don't want to push this baby on him. If I can get rid of it within the next few days, I can say I had a miscarriage and then everything'll be right. But I could never marry Henry - yes, it was Henry. He was kind to me, and I clung to him because I was so afraid, especially after the - well, you know what. I can't even bring myself to talk of it."

Two large tears welled up in her eyes, and her lips trembled. Putting a hand on Ruth's arm she said, "Help me, Ruth, please help me!"

And so she got her way. It was easy to find someone who knew 'someone', and arrangements were made for the next day. Emma went alone to a dirty-looking house in a mean street quite close to the docks. She shuddered as she glanced up at the house with its mud-splashed windows, behind which hung grey-looking lace curtains. At the window above a woman's face appeared, peered down at her and beckoned. "So she's the one," thought Emma, "Who'll do the 'job'." Climbing the torn, lino-covered stairs, she found a door open on the upper landing and heard a voice calling, "Come in, dearie, it's me you want to see. Close the door, I'm all ready for yer. Take yer coat off. My! that's what nice you're wearing. Pity yer got like this, you'll have to be careful next time!"

Emma's eyes roamed the room. In a dull grate a coal fire burned and smoked. The overmantel was dull and dusty; an alarm clock ticked away on the shelf, its glassless face quite brown from the perpetual smoking of the fire, and its bell covered with a spotted rust; an ashtray quite full of odds and ends, and a broken china dog stood either side. A faint gleam of the sun tried to struggle through the dirty window, and then within a few inches gave up, but not before the gathering dust was caught in its weak rays. There were four wooden chairs all filled with clothes, papers and shoes, one of which the woman was clearing and wiping with the end of her dull blue overall. In one corner was a bed with broken brass knobs, the centre of it sagging to the floor, and covered with a patchwork quilt of horrid colours. Beside the bed a cloth rug did its best to cover some of the torn oil cloth which once had stretched from end to end, but now had shrunk to reveal dirty floor boards. A small wooden table covered with dull American cloth held a chipped enamel bowl, a large piece of soap on a broken saucer, and a syringe. The woman was trying to smile, but at the same time endeavouring to hide her yellow broken dentures.

"I won't take long. Just get on the bed and do as I tell yer," Emma could hear, as the horror of the situation dawned on her. Poor they had always been, but never dirty like this. She glanced down at the woman's hands, yellow, rough, with filthy broken nails - and she was overcome with nausea.

"I can't," she said, "I can't!" this time almost with a scream. Frantically she opened her bag, flung three pound notes on the table and fled to the screams of abuse from the old hag. Regaining her balance once in the street, she thought, "What have I done? But I couldn't let that filthy woman touch me, I just couldn't. The dirt, it made me shudder. I've been used to something so different." And she thought of her body, loved and beloved both by Henry and Andrew. She would have to find some other way. Ruth would know. But quiet Ruth did not.

"The best thing for you, Emms, is to tell mother. You know since you're under age, you'll have to get her consent, and if she knows you're in the family way, her temper will fly but she'll be only too pleased to agree to your being married and save her disgrace in her neighbours' eyes."

Well, the outcome of it all was that soon, safely in her purse, Emma had her mother's written consent to marry, but not before she had met with a terrific onslaught. She was a dirty little bitch, and her mother knew she would come to this in the end. She always knew it, right from when she was born. A very nice prediction, Emma thought. She was called selfish, never thinking of them that brought her up, never sending home a penny to help, never giving a thought to them that denied themselves to give her full and plenty. (Emma wondered about the 'full and plenty'.) Here she was with beautiful clothes. How did she get them? Ah yes, of course, wasn't there evidence enough? On her back, of course, how else could a girl from the East End of London dress like that? It was, of course, all true, but looking back on the past year it didn't seem as crude as her mother tried to make it.

"I want to see this young man, my girl, so bring him here. I'll give him a piece of my mind, of course, if he is the one; but with clothes like those you've got on, it could be anyone. This chap, no doubt, is a bit of a simpleton and so you hooked him for it."

And on and on. To all this Emma kept quiet, biting the sharp retorts that rose frequently to her lips, remembering that Ruth had advised her, "Let mother say all she wants. Don't, for goodness' sake, answer her back. If you do, Ems, it will be all up for you."

The parting surprise was then too good to be true. "Here," said her mother, handing her a slip of paper with a name and address she had quickly written on it, "Here, if the bloke in the end won't marry you, go to this doctor. He brings things off very successfully. Anyway, I suppose if you do marry you'll come home and have the party here."

"Phew!" thought Emma as she boarded the bus to return to Ruth. What an unpredictable woman her mother was! One minute she would kill in her temper, and then the next she'd be ready to help. Ruth listened without comment.

By nature Emma was sensitive, and a little remorse began to creep into her as she thought of Henry, and of Andrew whom she had so deceived. She had lied to him in so many ways. First about her age. Now she'd have to tell him she had written consent to marry him. Then she'd have to confess she had told her mother and sister about her forthcoming marriage, and that they knew about the baby; and, of course, there was the thought of an abortion. How would he take that? Yes, one lie led to many. She must keep this all to herself.

When her conscience pricked, she would have to smother it. She could. She had got this far.

So having made up her mind, she 'phoned Andrew and told him she would be in town two days from then. She said she would bring Ruth to witness their wedding if he could find another witness. But Andrew, not wishing to encounter any of Emma's family, had replied that he had already arranged the witnesses, and they would be married in the little church in South Kensington by special licence.

And they were. Emma in the end had to confess that she had asked her mother for her written consent, but Andrew, it seemed, was so preoccupied with the final arrangements that he hardly noticed. They spent a week on the south coast, happy on the surface to be together again, yet inwardly cautious. Even Andrew's lovemaking seemed to take on another form, and both were becoming unhappy.

One night, as Emma lay in bed, she felt the first movement of the baby. Andrew was asleep. Instantly she wanted to wake him, but the knowledge that it was not Andrew's child, that she had bitterly deceived him, gave her reason to keep quiet. She twisted the ring, her wedding ring, which she had gained by such foul methods, and tears of self-pity welled up. She loved Andrew deeply, she told herself, <u>but</u>, said a little voice, "Not enough, not deeply enough to have been honest with him. You have played a rotten game." The voice continued. "Do something about it." "Do what?" she replied mentally, "I can't tell him the truth, he would leave me, I know he would."

"Well, remember the name and address your mother gave you," continued the voice. "Use it, go and see this person. You can get rid of this baby. Andrew will think it's a miscarriage, and you can begin all over again."

"Why not?" she answered as she drifted into sleep.

Andrew had decided not to return to London until he had written to his parents and made them aware that he was married. He had no intention of telling them when. He had a little cottage on the edge of Dartmoor, and there they went to live, to plan for the arrival of the baby. Emma fell in love with her new home, and was delighted with the village woman who came daily to look after them. The local doctor was called in to attend her, and after he had asked the usual questions he gave his verdict that the baby would arrive in five months' time. This news he quickly imparted to Andrew as he left, and it was a pale, silent man Emma joined in the lounge. Fear had entered her long before she had come downstairs, but sheer terror now assailed her as she met his piercing, cold blue eyes.

"Isn't there something you should tell me? Sit down!" he commanded, indicating an upright chair. "Sit down, Emma, before you fall down."

The silence was heavy; all was still; the evening song of the birds had ended, there was no sound of distant traffic, not a leaf moved on the trees; all was still, all were waiting with Andrew - Andrew, so different, a stranger; waiting-

She twisted a handkerchief, she straightened an imaginary crease in her dress, she looked towards the window, to the wall in front of her; the baby moved to remind her that he was what the trouble was all about. But she could not look at Andrew.

"Didn't you hear my question?" said the stranger before her, "Let me repeat it. Isn't there something you should tell me? My God, I can't believe it!" He moved closer to her, "Tell me, tell me the truth, and who is the father!"

"Andrew, Andrew!" she cried between bitter sobs that almost choked her, "Please, please forgive me. I loved you so much. I <u>do</u> love you. I didn't think this could happen. I didn't want to lose you. I'd do anything to keep you." Thinking of that sordid room, and the filthy woman, she sobbed harder. "Darling, what can I do?" Hysterically dropping on her knees, clasping his legs to her, she cried out "Help me, please. Oh, forgive me!"

He disengaged her arms, and pulled her to her feet. "Stop crying, Emma, sit down and tell me everything, from the the beginning. I want to know whose child it is, as it's certainly not mine, why you fostered it on me, and what you propose to do."

"To do! to do! I don't know. Yes, there was someone else before you made love to me, but I never loved him. I only love you!"

Between sobs she continued, "I didn't know when we went to Florence that I was pregnant, and when I did, I thought at first it was yours!"

"At first, what do you mean, at first? Did you know before we were married that this child wasn't mine?" Andrew went towards her and shook her so that her teeth rattled and the pins in her hair became loose, her hair falling like a black mantle over her shoulders. "Tell me, you little slut, you little whore!"

Somehow, in his fury, he heard her whisper, "Yes, yes I knew."

Quickly he strode from the room and mounted the stairs, and in some sort of stupor, Emma heard the opening and slamming of drawers, his heavy tread as he walked to and fro, and then he returned, stood just inside the door and very quietly said, "My solicitors will contact you. I'm leaving. Here's some money,"
He placed a number of notes on a side table. "Here's the address of my solicitor", and then a very hesitant "Goodbye!"

The front door closed with a bang. Emma sat there dazed, not thinking of anything, tears flowing steadily down her face. And so she sat well into the dusk. Somewhere a door creaked, and she became startled. She realised she was in the house alone; she couldn't stay. Andrew had gone. He had left her for good; he had said something about solicitors - she must get away, it was getting dark - but where, exactly where?

Into the hall she fled, and snatching her coat she almost flew through the door into the little drive that led to the road. She stumbled along, hurrying, breathless, sobbing, her hair flying behind her. A driving rain blotted out the little cottages she passed. She was getting drenched as she staggered and fell as her foot slipped on some wet leaves. Then some voices in the distance, she was being lifted, soothing tones, gentle hands, warm blankets wrapped her as her wet clothing was removed, a soft bed, a little glimmer from a lamp, and someone saying, "Call the doctor, and go down for her husband", and she was trying to say she had no husband, Andrew had gone, she had deceived him. Oh, and so many things more. But only her lips moved, and no sound came. A little prick in her arms, then blessed oblivion.

In the meantime, Andrew, in his righteous anger had caught the night train for London. His mind was confused, confused with so many things; his head ached and his hands trembled as he lit and threw away cigarette after cigarette. On his arrival he booked into an hotel, took a hot bath, and had some black coffee sent up to his room, and then flung himself on to the bed to think. His mind a little clearer, but with anger still consuming him, his first clear thought was that Emma had made an utter fool of him and had lied so well that he had believed all she'd said. He had been fascinated by her when they'd first met; he had continued to be when they met again. He knew that at first he had not really meant to take her to Florence, but when she had so readily accepted, he had not been able to resist her, and the lurking thought that there might be more to it than travelling together had come true. He had fallen for her, he had wanted her and she had been willing to give. He had been so excited by their love making. True, he had wondered if she had already had a lover, and was at first ready to ask. But he had fallen in love with her and she with him. The past was the past, he had thought, and I have had one too. Yet somehow, no matter how many affairs a fellow has had, he can not bear the thought that the woman he loves has lain in another's arms, and perhaps done the same thing and said the same words as she has said with him. Andrew winced as he thought of those nights. Her tenderness, her passion, they could not be false. She had said so many times that she loved him. The thought of her beauty, her charm, drifted over him like gossamer. His eyes were closed, he could feel her presence, he could catch a whiff of her perfume, he felt her lips upon his cheek, her face snuggled into his throat, and her hair like the lace of a mantilla covering her shoulders. Damn it! She was his wife. She bore his name. Why had he married her? Not because he loved her; he loved her without thought of marriage or the future. He'd married her because of the baby. He had had his doubts then; why, in heaven's name, had he not asked her? Why? Because he loved her, because she loved him, and he did not wish to know at the time about the others. Others, no that was unfair. Deceive him she had, and deliberately. But when? Had she not said that at first she did not know? She must have been terrified when she did. "Oh, Hell," he thought, flinging himself up from the bed, "I'll get dressed and go back. We'll work something out together."

He looked at his watch. Seven o'clock, what would she be doing? It was too early to leave the hotel. "Sit down," he thought, "try to be calm." He lit a cigarette, thinking of her, asleep perhaps, filling the white sheets with the smell of the provocative scent she always used. Memory stirred within him; he recalled the happiness they had both shared and relished to the full. Sometimes a wave of doubt had swept over him, even when he was most exalted; but it was muted, because he was caught up in the sunbeam of her love. At times, he felt a fore-boding that he might stumble into a chasm of doubt and wondering, but as each day came and went, the doubts receded, and slept, and Emma and Andrew were filled with overflowing contentment.

It was early evening when he arrived back at the cottage. All was quiet. He was met by Mrs Clarke, the woman who 'did' for them.

"Oh, sir!" she said in her soft Cornish voice, "I'm indeed so glad you've come home - Mrs Craig isn't well, the doctor..."

But Andrew had bounded up the stairs and quietly entered the bedroom. Emma lay asleep, her face turned towards him. He tiptoed closer and looked at her. She had no colour, her breathing was very quiet, and it was only the gentle rise and fall of her bosom that told him she was alive. He was alarmed and quietly left the room.

Mrs Clarke told him how Mrs Craig had been out the last evening, was caught in the rain, stumbled and fell. Fortunately it was near Mrs Clarke's cottage; they had taken her in and sent for a doctor when they realised she had fainted. When the doctor saw that Mrs Craig was becoming excitable as she came to, he gave her an injection, brought her home, and Mrs Clarke had been with her ever since. The doctor had called again, was not satisfied with her condition and had given her a sedative and said she would sleep through the night. He said she must have complete rest because her condition would perhaps cause a miscarriage. Now that Mr Craig had returned, Mrs Clarke hoped that if she left him some supper, she could go home.

Barely hearing, Andrew said, "Yes, thank you", poured himself a stiff whisky, and took it upstairs. He seated himself near the bedroom window, gazing at the stars as they began to twinkle one by one. In a little while he quietly undressed, wrapped himself in his robe, then took a spare blanket from a cupboard and settled on a small divan, prepared to watch over Emma through the night. He had fallen sleep as dawn was breaking, when Emma, gradually waking and her vision becoming clearer was astonished to see him. Was it a continuation of a dream? It must be, because he had left her in such anger! She looked again harder, and realised it was he; a happy smile hovered around her lips; she turned, closed her eyes and in a short while was asleep again. When she woke again, Andrew stood beside her, freshly groomed, a look of consternation across his face. They both looked deeply at each other, muted with embarrassed emotion. Clearing his throat, he quietly said, "Emma, Baby, forgive me - I love you, that's all I can say." He gathered her into his arms, but she withdrew.

"We must talk this over. I've done so much harm to you, and I realise a little of what you must feel. I have the name of a doctor who can cancel this out for me."

He looked at her incredulously, "Whatever are you thinking about? It's dangerous and criminal to do such a thing! You must forget it!"

"But we never shall. I mustn't have this baby; it's not yours; all your life you'll remember, more even than I. You have a family to be proud of, and should only have your own blood in it."

"Darling, darling, we'll argue this forever, so we must learn to live with it, if we're to be happy. If you have an abortion, since I know how sensitive, and loving you are, for the rest of your life you'll regret it, and even blame me in some sort of way. I realise I love you, love you more than I ever thought I could, and so we'll see this through together. From now on we only think of him as a little Craig. We must love him and give him the privileges of our union." He put his hand across her mouth gently as she was about to interrupt him. "No. don't speak, hear me out. I'll ask no questions of you, and you'll never refer to this time again. In time it will become dim. Don't ever think of me as generous. I'm selfish, I'm here because I can't be without you. We'll have other children too, and make this a very happy family."

They looked deeply at each other. He knew that he was no better than the other fellow. The tables could have been reversed if he had not loved her so much. But she was his wife now.

And looking at Andrew, Emma understood. Resting her head against him, she murmured, "Darling, there's nothing I can say except thank you." The tears flowed freely , partly for him, but mostly for the little man child that stirred within her.

Chapter Nine

A little boy lay in his bed watching the flames from the fire leap and frolic on the ceiling; the wind and rain on the nursery windows blew a merry tune, and there were voices in the distance. Doors were opening and shutting, and Nanny said to go to sleep because Mummy and Daddy were having a party and wouldn't be able to come and see him. But Carlos knew differently; Mummy especially would never let him go to sleep without seeing her little boy, her Carlos. There were times, of course, when she might have to be away, but she and Carlos had such a perfect understanding between them that when this happened he would know that, although he couldn't see her, she was still very close to him, and he would go to sleep contentedly. Dadda, of course, was different. He was a man, kind, loving, but a little remote. He and Mummy loved each other very, very much, and Carlos bathed in the radiance of their love. He waited tonight a little breathlessly, especially for his darling Mummy. She had promised to be in her beautiful party dress, and he would see on her throat the lovely milky beads Dadda had given her, and the small ones in her ears. Hadn't Dadda said on Mummy's birthday, as he put the string around her neck, "Happy birthday, Baby. A few pearls for the greatest pearl in my life", and Carlos remembered the lovely kisses they had given each other. He had been swooped up into Dadda's arms, and Dadda had said:

"Always love your Mummy, old chap. She's wonderful to us!" and Carlos had felt his chest swell with love and pride as she stood before them, beautiful, her eyes the most lovely in the world to him, lips that revealed her white, even teeth, fascinating even to a little boy.

Mummy had said in a very tight voice, "And you, my sweet, love Dadda for he is the most wonderful man!" and somehow there had been a silence, broken by a funny laugh from Dadda, who'd said, "Come, let's not be serious. It's Mummy's birthday, and we're going to celebrate."

That was a little while ago. He lay in his lovely warm bed, cosy, and snuggled down further, thinking he could lie there for ever and ever. But he mustn't go to sleep yet. He looked around him, and in the firelight he could see his room, large with beautiful nursery rhyme paper on its walls. He knew the curtains were dull gold and green, drawn across two large windows that had bars across "so that little boys wouldn't fall out." He knew his feet buried themselves in the red carpet, and that his canopy was all beautiful colours - like Jacob's coat, Mummy said. The furniture stood out white and gold, and the fire flames flickered on the door just across from his bed. "Yes, I must keep my eyes open for Mummy." Sleep was just around the corner, and would have overtaken him if the door hadn't just then gently opened and the light from outside revealed her as she turned, closed the door and came over to him. He sprang up and nearly into her arms, but with a little gentle push she said:

"Not tonight, sweetheart. Look!" And switching on the bed-side light, she continued, "Look, I'm in all my party clothes, and my hair is so very tidy!"

She stood back for him to see. He was fascinated. He saw her beautiful black hair dressed, he did not know how, but it rested on the nape of her neck. Her bare throat and the top of her breasts, which he could see, rose above her white brocaded body. He could see with delight two tiny electric lights in her ears, and on her fingers. She laughed when he told her, and she explained they were diamonds.

"I like them anyway," he said, and again she gave a little laugh. Mummy was always laughing, and always singing too.

"Now, my sweet, I know you've been waiting a long time for me, but I hurried to take my bath and dress before you went to sleep. Let me hear your prayers and tuck you up. Tomorrow I'll tell you all about the party." Carlos, catching his hands together, began "Our Father..."

But he would not be hurried. He had waited this long, and his audience was not complete. "Just wait for Dadda, Mummy, he told me he would be all dressed up, too, and I would like to see him. Tell me again, who's coming?"

"Grandpa and Grandma, Auntie Deborah and Uncle Francis, Colonel and Mrs Durand, Lord George Kemp and the lady he's going to marry, Isobel Trafford."

"Lots of people, Mummy. Can I see them now? Can I see Grandpa and Grandma - please?"

"Now hush, darling - oh, here's Dadda," said Emma, turning towards Andrew. "He won't say his prayers until you come."

She took Carlos' hands and placed them together, and he bent both his knees and began once again: "Our Father..." ending with "God bless Mummy, and Dadda, and Nanna..." So it went on, Carlos thinking the longer the prayer lasted, the longer they would stay with him and the more he could feast his eyes on the little bright lights on Dadda's shirt front, the same as Mummy's bright lights.

"That's enough, old chap. Down you go to sleep; the sooner you sleep, the quicker the morning will come, and we can go riding with your new pony." A hearty kiss upon his cheek, then, "Come along, darling, I want to hear your news before the others come." Then Mummy all sweet-smelling, bent and kissed him, oh, ever so nicely, and tucked him up and followed Dadda to the door. Carlos heard Dadda say in a loud undertone, "How lovely you look, Baby, in the firelight, ravishing!" He kissed her full on the mouth. "I wish it was all over, and we were alone..."

Emma gave a happy little chuckle and pushed him out of the door saying, "Later, you old silly. Come down to the library and I'll tell you my news while we have a drink."

Handing her a Martini, Andrew said with light expectancy, "What did Dr Kemp tell you - what was his verdict?"

Emma lowered her glass, and without any gentle approach to the disappointing news she had to give, abruptly said, "Again, I'm sorry to say - oh, hell, darling, am I always going to give you the same news? Kemp said, as he did last time, that Mr Hilary's verdict was correct I'm perfectly normal, as he's already told you you are. But, I'm so very, very anxious for another child that instead of conceiving, my over anxious state makes conceiving less likely. Really, I can't understand it. I'm healthy, enjoy, more than enjoy, our sex life, and yet when I'm certain that I've conceived - missing my period, the sickness, the swelling of my breasts are actually happening - due to this over anxiousness, they're all false. How ironic! When I didn't want..."

Andrew drew her quickly to him. "Baby, never say anything we agreed to forget. Five years ago we had a darling little boy. We must be prepared to wait until nature takes her course. She can be very fickle, you know. Anyway, put your arms around me, tell me you love me, as I love you. I never tire of hearing it. Dearest Emma, how happy we are, the three of us."

The door bell rang, and the butler's footsteps rang on the marbled hall floor. Emma released herself, recovered her equilibrium, and softly said, "In my heart I often think of you as Jacob, the Biblical Jacob, who waits and serves seven years for Rachel before he can make her his wife. Who knows, perhaps in two more years you may be rewarded." He could make no reply, for they both stepped forward to greet his parents, and the rest of the guests followed.

Andrew and Emma regularly gave dinner parties while in London. It was extraordinary how quickly Emma had settled into Andrew's way of life. His family had been very upset when they had first learned of his marriage and the birth of the baby. Andrew had timed everything perfectly and he and Emma were back at the villa in Fiesole before he acquainted them with the news. Lady Craig was extremely upset, her husband more silent on the affair. But they both decided not to make too much comment until they met their new daughter-in-law and grandchild. The baby was three months old when they went out and paid their first visit. It was very evident to them that Emma did not come from the same social background as they did. They noted, too, that her speech had the intonation of an East London accent; but their outward calm and warm composure, her loveliness and the obvious fact that she and Andrew were very much in love seemed to satisfy them. They felt, when introduced to Carlos, that there was a nervousness about the young couple, and later they decided it could be because Emma might have been pregnant by Andrew before their marriage. Hence a hasty, secret wedding. How like his mother, and what a beautiful child he was! They felt proud looking at him and even though Lady Craig, full of ambition, tradition and snobbery, had felt aggrieved that all this had occurred unknown to them and she had been deprived of a fashionable London wedding, she was at heart a generous woman and a loving mother, and cared about her sons' happiness. Her husband was philosophical. He had a roving eye, and without hesitation mentally embraced this lovely new daughter - the future Lady Craig.

Dinner was a very pleasant affair. The men were enjoying their port and cigars while the ladies waited for them to join them. Emma sat behind the coffee tray performing the usual duties of a hostess. She was always so composed and confident, and was regarded as a perfect hostess.

"I read this morning," said Lady Craig, taking her coffee from Emma, "an obituary to the Dowager Lady Gavannah. I had heard she was none too well and intended to call on her, so I was very shocked to see she had died yesterday. She was very keen to help the Tommies during the war, and was regarded very highly for her charitable work. Did you know her, Mrs Durand? A thorough aristocrat!"

"No. Most of my married life has been spent in India, and one loses touch with so many people. Not that I should ever had been in Lady Gavannah's set. She was elderly, I read, withdrawn, and I'm sure even if we had lived in London all our lives I should never have been accepted. My people were in trade, you know."

Isobel Trafford laughed. She was the daughter of the Duke of Stanbury. Her family were extremely wealthy, having inherited a vast fortune from an American maternal grandmother. She had a sister and two brothers. Isobel Trafford was tall, fair, had a willowy figure and the features of a thoroughbred. At one time Lady Craig had wishfully thought that Andrew might have been interested enough to marry her. They had grown up together, attended all the children's parties together in the same set, and were very used to each other. And there it began and ended. Isobel was at first surprised at Andrew's choice of a wife, but kept that to herself. As a frequent visitor to the house, she has succumbed to the charm of Emma, and Emma had responded. They were now very firm friends and so intimate that Isobel, without causing any hurt or giving any outward offence, had assisted Emma socially and with tact had given some very necessary advice. Both women had been circumspect enough not to let Andrew know, and neither had really openly admitted that Isobel was launching Emma. Emma, loving Andrew as she did, was eager to be the perfect hostess and the kind of wife she knew Andrew should have. Isobel had recently become engaged to Lord George Kemp, himself the second son of an impoverished earl. He was ten years older than Isobel, was something on the Exchange and a keen cricketer and, like most men of his age and standing, could take his liquor. He was known to say at his London club, "It's an excellent sign of one's virility to play cricket and take one's liquor." Lord George Kemp had sown his wild oats in full. He had skimmed the edges of more than one society scandal and skated to safer, firmer surfaces. Before the ice cracked beneath the weight of his high adventures and philandering with the opposite sex, he decided to settle down with someone of his own choice, someone who would not demand too intimate a relationship, someone who would not hold the reins too tightly. He had proposed to, and to his surprise been accepted by the lovely creature who had been his dinner partner at one of the small private parties given by the Prince of Wales. "All very exciting, old chap," he had said next day to a business associate. "She's a perfect filly!"

And now the perfect filly was laughing at the thought of the dead Dowager. Turning to Rose Durand she said,"Oh yes, the poor old darling was very eccentric! She always wanted to know if people were in Debrett before she would meet them. She used to hold her At Homes once a month, and very stuffy affairs they were. I literally shrank when she looked me up and down, with her lorgnette perched on her high-bridged nose." Here Isobel imitated the action, to the merriment of the others.

The men entered, and the conversation changed. Andrew gave Emma a warm, loving glance and seated himself beside Isobel.

"We shall, I hope, be having news of your wedding soon, Isobel. Don't wait until we go to Florence and then expect us to rush back. You know we always enjoy staying at the villa for three months, and in that time I can do quite a lot of business with wine merchants."

Looking around at everyone Isobel said, "George and I are not in too much of a hurry to marry. We have to find a house, both here and in the country. We're having some difficulty in getting what we need, and mother tells me the servant problem gets worse. So go to your villa, Andrew. We won't be marrying yet."

"Don't take Andrew too seriously, Isobel. Wherever we are we'll be here for your wedding." Emma, having given the menfolk their coffee, rose and opened the music on the piano. "Will you play something for us, Father?"

"Of course, my dear, if you will sing for us."

On the opening bars Emma sang from <u>The Dashing White Sergeant!</u>

"When I had a beau for a soldier who'd go
Should you think I'd say no?
No, no, not I.
For a soldier who'd go do you
Think I'd say no
No, no, no, no, no, no, not I.
When his red coat I saw not a tear would it draw.
But I'd give him a cheer for his bravery."

"Very lovely, my dear. I enjoy accompanying your songs." Turning to Andrew, Lord Craig said, "I think you were quite right to encourage Emma to study music. I feel sure if she'd done it earlier she could have made singing a career. But then," catching Emma's hand, "we should have been deprived, no doubt, of a lovely daughter and our grandchild."

Emma turned to cross the room and join Andrew and Isobel. She always suffered on these occasions; not even Andrew knew how much.

The evening passed pleasantly and quickly. Finally guests had all gone and they were alone having a final drink before retiring.

"How kind your parents are to me, darling! They both knew when they first met me that I was some little East Ender, and yet they've accepted me, made me feel one of the family..."

"Emma, don't always refer to what's past. I've told you so many times before. It's a time which is best forgotten. I believe I told you this when we first met in Paris." He took her hand and looked very deeply into her eyes. "We are man and wife. We love each other, and suit each other admirably. Now, tell me what happened this afternoon when Dr Kemp called."

Emma settled back into her chair, feeling tired and inwardly miserable. She had so wanted another child, a family infact. Each time she felt this is it. She soon became aware that once again she was to be disappointed. Visits on these occasions to the family doctor always brought forth the same remarks:

"You're perfectly healthy and so is your husband, Mrs Craig. You're simply over anxious, and nature has a way of deluding one. Give it time. Don't rush things. You're very fit."

Finally, when it seemed evident to Emma that this time the dream was really coming true, and she was sure of fulfilling her desire to give Andrew the child they both wanted, the disappointment became even greater to bear when once again she realised she had failed him.

"Oh! he called to give Mr Hilary's verdict - I had told Kemp I wanted to be examined by a specialist, and this is what I get for my pains. First you, and then me on his couch, being turned almost inside out, and the same: "You're perfectly healthy and normal, and must have patience. So there you are." She twisted a handkerchief vigorously.

"Well, Baby, I feel I have nothing to say; I feel inadequate too, so let's go to bed. You must be tired. You were lovely tonight, a perfect little hostess." He pulled her up, clasping her closely to him. "Shall we go?" And he repeated in an inviting tone, "Shall we go, my darling?"

As they undressed and prepared for bed they talked of the holiday in Italy. Carlos could remain with his Nanny in Andrew's parents' home. They loved having him, and the child was very happy with them. He understood that his parents would soon return. Emma for her part would rather have remained in England with him, but she had quickly learnt that the people into whose class she had married did not take their children wherever they went. Servants were entrusted with the care of one's offspring, and so Emma had tried to stifle the possessiveness which was part of her upbringing. True, children in poorer circumstances roamed the streets, were often neglected and ill cared for, but mothers, when roused, showed the fierce aggressiveness of the tiger when their young were attacked. There was no need to show any of this to Carlos, who had been born into a different world from Emma. Yet in her heart, deep and well rooted, was an all-absorbing love of the child. She was conscious of what she had done to him; she was conscious of the fact that all along the line she was cheating - cheating her mother and father-in-law of a rightful heir, cheating Carlos, and most of all Andrew. Here she was, young, desirable and healthy, enjoying the life she now lived, responsive at all times to Andrew's love-making - in fact often the first to show desire - and yet, in the end, failing him.

Getting into bed beside her and switching off the light, he gathered her into his arms and said with a little catch in his throat, "Goodnight, my darling. Go to sleep. Don't worry, and everything will be fine. We have each other and -" As she was about to speak, he added, "and we have one child. We must be content."

Time passed quickly, outwardly pleasant. Isobel was married, Christmas came and went, and spring once again shimmered on the horizon. They spent a couple of weeks in Paris, doing the usual things, Andrew contacting business acquaintances. Then they travelled to Florence and to their rented villa in Fiesole. Maria was still with them, caring for the house when they were away, fussing and mothering them both when they were there. The beauty of the surrounding hills always beckoned Emma and she motored to them whenever she could. She learned the language and was able to speak with their guests in their own tongue. Among the people living in the sumptuous villas on the slopes going down to Florence were artists and literary people, of whom many were their guests to lunch and dinner. These meals were delightful and prolonged. Food and wine were not only enjoyed, but were one of the main subjects of conversation. Emma was elated with these people and their arts. She breathed the air and trod in the footsteps of Shelley, Byron, Dickens and the like. One couple had become their very firm friends. They lived not far from the peaceful terrace of St Francis. The ancient tiny monastery held a great fascination for Emma, and she would roam the cloisters and tiny cells, asking innumerable questions of a very ancient monk whose job it was to show visitors round. Cristina and Lorenzo were a charming couple. He was an artist of the first water, and Cristina was a very literary person; many of her novels had been acclaimed as far afield as America, and she also had a good following in England. Lorenzo, like most Italians, was not tall, but broad shouldered with jet black hair, large deep brown eyes, a good nose and a gentle mouth. His hands were somewhat squat and his fingertips square. They were good hands, that reproduced in paint the beauty he saw all around him, and wove it on his canvasses. His temperament was even, good-natured and, like most Italians, ready for fun. Cristina was different, slightly taller than her husband, slender, with no part of her body revealing that she had had three bouncing daughters in quick succession. The girls were at school in England, and were all in their teens. To the person who first met her she gave the impression that she was retiring and a little vague. Perhaps she was. But when she had decided you were a person she wished to know, and to be acquainted with, the veils disappeared and she revealed her warmth, her lovely smile, and her interest. Emma enjoyed all of this. The Ferraris had a villa in Venice and usually in late summer went there for the 'season', to participate in the Royal Regatta, and to enjoy the plays and concerts at the Goldini, and the opera at La Fenice. They had invited Emma and Andrew to be their guests. Excited, they had accepted, but before going they had returned to England to spend a few months with Carlos.

Isobel had invited them to her country home in Norfolk for a weekend house party. It was a beautiful house in wooded country, not many miles from Newmarket. The house was full of guests, and servants too. Many had stayed on from Newmarket races, and the conversation was very "horsey", and not much in Emma's line. So she had got away from them and wandered into the garden with a book. She had noticed, when passing across the wide drive, some chauffeur-driven cars. Just now a chauffeur was lightly dusting his car, no doubt waiting for its owner, but Emma hardly glanced that way. If she had, she would have noticed the eyes that looked straight at her, the body that stiffened almost to a statue. For this was none other than Henry. But happily she tripped on, walked through the garden into some meadowland, and settled on the grass beneath a huge oak tree. Happily she opened her book and began to read and was soon lost in the violent and tragic love of Cathy and Heathcliff in Wuthering Heights'. She heard no footsteps over the velvety grass, but something told her to glance a little to one side, and she saw a pair of shining shoes, men's shoes, nearly touching. Her eyes for a few seconds were hypnotised, and with a great effort she raised her lids and let them travel from the shoes upwards, over the legs clad in a uniform of navy blue, and then into the eyes of Henry, who had bent to draw her to her feet. She opened her mouth, but no sound came, arms crushed her to a broad chest, kisses rained down on her mouth, her eyes, her neck, until breathlessly he let her go. Fear, stark raging fear beset her, her mind darting this way and that, her cheek now pressed to his buttoned uniform, still within his eager grasp. Then, a little breathlessly and with emotion, he said, as he put her away from him, "Emma, where have you been? I would have known you in a thousand years. Don't look so startled; I'm real, I'm just the same! I've never stopped loving you, never stopped looking, and never given up hope."

She looked to the left, to the right; there was no escape. This was Henry. This was the moment she had been dreading all these years. She knew, she knew it would all catch up with her. Andrew, Carlos, oh, God! what should she do?

Holding her by the shoulders and looking deeply at her, with a nervous little laugh he asked, "Where do you live? What do you do? You look so beautiful, your clothes are lovely." He brushed a hand over her brow and down to the nape of her neck. "Still the same beautiful hair and you wear it just the same way. This is how I always remembered you." Bending now, he kissed her with some of his old fervour. "Do you still go to bed with your hair in a long plait? Remember how I used to wind it round my neck?"

The fear that had trapped her now released her hitherto paralysed tongue. "Stop it! Stop it, please! Take your hands off me! Please, I beg of you, go away!" She raised her left hand to push him away from her. He laughingly clutched it in his two, holding it rather firmly.

"Don't be silly, Ems, no one will see you from here. I know you're surprised, even shocked to see me, but I'm quite real." Bending to kiss her with more passion than before, pressing her firmly against the tree trunk, he pushed a hand on to her mouth, forcing open her clenched teeth and probing her mouth with his tongue. She struggled fiercely to free her hand, and using the other she did so. Henry gave a gasp as something scratched his hand. He looked down and saw a ring glittering on her third finger. Quietly he lifted her and once again, saw the wedding ring and the circle of diamonds above it.

"So, you're married. When? To whom?"

She nodded. "I've been married nearly six years. Please go away. What happened between us is past and forgotten." (It was, she thought, when daily she had a human reminder?) "Go away, Henry; forget you've met me. I don't want my husband to know about you. Besides, we have a little boy and we are all very happy together." She bent down to retrieve her book. She made to pass him, but he stood in her way, tall, firm and strong, with a granite-like look. All love had left him, he was just waiting now. He had to know.

"Who have you married, Emma, how old is your little boy?" He drew her close to him, searching her eyes, her face, the lips that were so ready to lie. Quietly, very quietly, he said close to her ear, "Does he love you as I do, are you the same with him in bed as you were with me? Tell me, tell me!"

She struggled and freed herself, and as she hastened from him said over her shoulder, "Go away, please leave me alone!"

But in her hurry, his voice did not reach her. "Never, Emma, never!"

Chapter Ten

There was quite a bit, by careful enquiry, that Emma discovered about Henry. He was a footman to Isobel and George Kemp since they had married and taken this country house. He was regarded as a perfect servant, quiet and reliable. He drove the car whenever he was needed to do so, and he had just returned from London where he had met George and brought him home. George was rather a reckless driver, and Isobel was always eager for Henry to drive him. He had had good references from two of his previous employers. As Emma was very intimate with Isobel it was easy to ask questions about the staff. That night at dinner, the meal took an eternity to end for Emma. There was Henry, quietly performing his duties; never for a moment, even to <u>her</u>, was he other than the perfect servant. He followed the butler around the table, he took coffee to the drawing-room when the ladies settled, awaiting the men. He closed the curtains, emptied the ashtrays, performed all the little duties of a well-trained servant, but Emma wasin such a whirl that she could have screamed.

With the plea of a headache she excused herself and said she would go to bed. Henry opened the door for her, and for just a split second their eyes met. Andrew found her lying on the bed with her face buried in her pillow.

"Are you not well, darling?" he enquired as he turned her over to face him and, putting a hand on her forehead, he said "You're quite feverish. Let me help you to undress, take some aspirins and if you feel no better I'll ask Isobel to call her doctor."

"No, no! just leave me. I feel a bit under the weather - perhaps I have a cold on the way" she sat up twisting a handkerchief in her hot fingers, "Go down," she told Andrew "I can soon go to bed and then I'll be asleep in no time." She gave a little watery smile as she said it.

"We're just waiting for the tables to be put up for Bridge. If I play, I won't be able to come up again until the game's over. I think

I'll cull out, and stay here with you," getting up from the bed, he tried to unhook her pearls.

"How can I get rid of him? thought Emma. I want to be alone. I want to think; I can't tell him, I've hurt him enough. Her mind was racing, Oh, go away, Andrew, go away! Yet calmly, deadly so, she coaxed aloud, I'll be perfectly all right once I'm in bed and the light's out. Go down, dear, offer my apologies, and enjoy your game. Kiss me goodnight now, I'll certainly be asleep when you come up."

Reluctantly he kissed her, and left her to her own bewildering thoughts. She sat before the mirror in a dream, brushing and plaiting her hair. Mechanically she attended to the rest of her toilet and got into bed. The darkness would be more kind to her bewildered mind and her throbbing head. She stretched out and blotted out the light. Terror besieged her. Everything was closing in on her. What could she do to save Carlos, to shield Andrew? Henry would discover the truth, she had no doubt. Would he try to claim the boy? People, incidents, places, all tumbled through her bewildred mind. She must fight, she could deny everything to Henry, but not to Andrew if he ever got to know of Henry. Henry! Isobel's servant! But what had Emma been? A servant like him; she must not forget that; she mustn't think of Henry with disdain. He had wanted to marry her - remember? - and she had only laughed at him. He had been so kind to her when she had been alone and frightened. Think kindly of him, Emma, and if anyone is to suffer, let it be you, only you, you can bear it, you can, you can! she told herself; but almost like lightning she knew it would be impossible almost impossible, for had she not Henry to ward off, Carlos and Andrew to shield?

Sleep began to overcome her, and she drifted away into a world of love and happiness. There was dear Andrew beneath the olive trees in the garden of their Italian villa, and he was holding her gently, stroking her hair, calling her love names, kissing her eyes, her throat, the kisses becoming insistent, his lips forcing apart her teeth and his tongue exploring her mouth. She succumbed to it all, and wondered, her eyes closed against his face, how he could explore her body and yet hold her so firmly in his arms. She gave herself to her beloved, she rose above the clouds higher and higher, and then spent herself. "Darling!" she murmured, and suddenly she was back again in her bed, but not alone. Someone, something was bending over her, a hand was on her breast travelling downwards; she struggled, her mouth was crushed by firm lips, and she knew, she knew! Henry! God, what was she to do! His mouth travelled to an ear and he whispered, "Be quiet. No one will move from the drawing room for hours. Let me have you, Emma, I'm crazy for you, you belong to me, not the man you married. Keep still, you had no thought for me, you left me - I always wanted you, I've had no other." She was struggling violently, but he was big and strong. "Come," he said, "you never did struggle, if I remember right, you often asked for it. Come on, let me see if he has kept you in good training." He was over her. Swiftly she raised a knee and jerked into his groin. With a groan of intense pain he flopped, and in a flash Emma was out of bed, putting on her robe and switching on the light.

"Henry, go now, or else I'll ring for someone to come, and that would need some explaining on your part."

Breathlessly he rose. hooking his trousers, and looking deeply at her. "You won't ring, Emma, for you'd be the one doing the explaining. I'm sorry I came to you this way, but all evening I've been crazy with thoughts of you. I'll go, but before I do, let me tell you that I've been making enquiries about the boy from <u>your</u> chauffeur. I'll tell you what I think some other time. But now I've found you, I won't give up. I know you, Emma, hot as ever. You were enjoying me before you woke up, and in the future I'll make you come to me, want me! Don't worry, I'll have you!"

He left the room. She tumbled back into bed and in the light she thought and remembered, and was ashamed that he had excited her. Pictures of the past floated before her eyes.

Within a week Emma and Andrew were in Venice. Carlos and his Nanny were with Andrew's parents. The Ferraris were perfect hosts and a round of entertainment began. Thoughts of Henry were pushed aside, and in the whirl and excitement of Venetian life Emma managed not to think of him. She fell completely in love with Venice. They arrived in the late morning by train, and leaving the station, followed by porters with their luggage, they took the Vaporetto which plunged its way into the Grand Canal, beneath the Rialto Bridge. The Palaces on either side with their faded blues and browns and reds gave a welcome, as did the gondolas, some passing, some drawn up to the mooring poles which were of brilliant striped colours. They alighted at the Crecademia and were met. The villa was very lovely. Emma was intrigued that on one side the canal lapped its waters. On entering, she saw a small courtyard filled with tubs of flowers, and in the centre a small fountain spraying from the organ of a stone urchin. The living apartments were on the upper floors, it was explained, because in the winter the canal swelled and often rose high up the inner walls. The rooms were long and spacious. The bedroom they were given had two very large windows which overlooked the Grand Canal. The shutters were closed to keep out the midday sun. The walls were covered with satin striped paper. Thick rugs were strewn across a marble floor. The bed was huge and canopied, the furniture glit, and an enormous crystal chandelier hung in the centre with matching wall lights. Emma explored the bathroom and dressing room with its enormous wardrobes. Refreshed, they joined their hosts in the beautiful salon and were introduced to the Lorenzo's parents, who would also be in Venice for the season.

It was wonderful to wake each morning to unusual sounds - the noisy quarrelsome voices of the gondoliers, with their straw beribboned hats at a particular angle, their oars on their shoulders as they made their way to gondolas near St Marks Square; the birds caged in glit aviary on the verandah just across the narrow lane as the sun peeped for a while between the tall buildings - and not far away, St Mark's and the Doges Palace. The Ferraris family owned a gondola, and had in their service a gondolier. He sang as he swung them into the Grand Canal, and then into the Lagoon. The hub of life was intense. St Mark's Square was filled each day with tourists and citizens alike. They would sit in a maze of chairs and tables outside the famous Florian Cafe, idling way the morning, drinking coffee, listening to the music of an orchestra, and then, when weary of that, wander into the Merceria, losing themselves in the sumptuous shops with their display of looking glasses, gold Venetian furniture, lace and jewellery. They would eventually find themselves near the Rialto Bridge, notice the time had passed quickly, and then hasten over many bridges to be back at the villa promptly for lunch. This, amidst much talk, would take more than two hours, and Andrew easily fell in with the custom of the siesta. In the dusk of the evening they would watch the lights gradually appear one by one. Sometimes their hosts would entertain at home, sometimes they would go with Emma and Andrew and dine with friends in one of the beautiful hotels. Emma discovered the good nature of the Venetians, their love of art, their love of pomp.

One night they attended a concert in the courtyard of the Doges Palace - the moonlight played into it, the air was warm, a gentle breeze wafted across from the Grand Canal as the orchestra from the Fenice played Chopin and Mendelssohn. The emotions of both Emma and Andrew were at high pitch as they wended their way back across the piazzala. The early morning air was filled with laughter and song. Somewhere the Ferraris followed, but Emma and Andrew hastily and silently hurried forward. Emotion like this they had not experienced before; quickly they bade their hosts goodnight, and eagerly they sought each other. Few words had passed between them, each keyed to the very limit, the world forgotten, the world lost, only each other, clinging, grasping, breathless, their love silent, just the rhythm of their bodies and the fierceness as they clung together, and just as both were ready to give, Andrew said, "Love me, Baby?" and she replied, "Yes, yes, I do, my darling, please, oh, please give me a baby!" and suddenly the picture of Carlos together with Henry came before her closed eyes, and fiercer than ever she clung to him, and louder and louder came her silent plea, "Oh, give me a baby, give me, give me!"

Afterwards they lay side by side holding each other's hands, and he turned to her after a while. "Emma, darling, I love you more than I can tell you. I love you more each day, don't ever stop loving me." She was surprised that his cheeks were wet as they came close to her. She prayed for strength to love and protect her family, to keep them free from harm, and as his head rested upon her shoulder and he fell asleep, she lay to watch the new dawn, a new day, and perhaps a new life would awaken within her. She had deceived him, she had deceived Henry, she had cheated. "If there is to be suffering in tbe future, "she prayed, "let me be the one, let me alone bear the cross."

Days of pleasure, full of delight, glided by in Venice. Cristina became very attached to Emma. There was something about Emma that drew people. She had character and a strong personality, and most people who became acquainted with her wished to know her more. Her laughter was infectious, her interest in everything around her was gratifying to any who were entertaining her. She was not shy to let the world know that after seven years of marriage she was very much in love with Andrew. They would indicate by a quick glance across the room that they were aware of each other's presence. They caught the imagination and the love of the romantic Venetians whom they met. Emma's beauty increased. She knew how to dress, her large hazel eyes were always shining, and her mouth still had the full provocative underlip, which showed just the tiniest bit of her white teeth that seemed to rest upon it, as though she was just going to let out a little gasp of surprise. Her ears were small and well shaped, and mostly adorned by tiny pearls. Her brow was broad, surrounded by astonishing black hair, Andrew called it blue black. She never changed its style, which seemed to help build up her character. All this Cristina saw as Emma sat across the saloon from her. It was evident too that Emma's rounded figure, youthful now, would put on unwanted flesh if she were not careful in her later life. But she was young and that was not noticeable now.

"Tell me, Emma, do you have beauty treatment for your skin?" Cristina asked half shyly, with the gesture of hands familiar to Italians.

Emma laughed, and was surprised at the question. "No, Cristina, just plain soap and water. I seldom use make up, perhaps in the evening a lipstick and dusting of powder."

"I envy such a skin. We Italians look very brown perhaps in the summertime, but during the winter I always think we look a little - how do you call it - sallow?"

Lorenzo's mother had joined them and had heard the conversation. "I always think the English have beautiful skin, but yours is remarkable, cara mia; you must take care the sun does not spoil it. Tell me, why are the English so solemn? We like laughter and music. We also enjoy, very much, good food. I have spent many months in England during my life and I find hotels are not good. Everything closes early. People go around serious, never speaking to each other."

Emma, like the East End urchin she was, had a powerful sense of loyalty. She knew the pangs of hunger, the lack of essentials, the misery of poverty, the appalling cold, when there was no coal in the winter. The quarrels which arose in households that lacked these things often continuous, caused by frayed nerves, people driven to desperation, made into animals. But despite this, they were British, and came forward to defend their King and Country directly the need arose. To grumble and complain at their betters, or those more fortunate was their prerogative, but let any outsider criticise, and they rose in union to defend. The Crown, the Empire were supreme. And though in the past few years Emma had been fortunate enough to live on the other side, full and plenty, content, she knew that fundamentally they were all the same - British to the backbone.

"I believe we are, as a nation, not understood one little bit. In my country there's a great deal of poverty and hardship. I see it here too. The Italians seem to be full of happiness and laughter, full of music, but in my opinion that's only to be found amongst those with full and plenty. In the poorer classes you find laughter does not come quite so easily. Your poor, like ours, would be very happy to enjoy the good food you talk about. But circumstances deny them. Continually in England people are striving for better conditions, and they <u>will</u> come. Our national character is reserved, and we give the impression to the rest of the world that we're indifferent to everything that goes on around us. But directly we are challenged we rise, grit our teeth into adversity and without more ado, dispatch the enemy, whoever he might be. Hence our label 'John Bull'. Remember the fierce endeavour of the last war? Of <u>all</u> wars in which we participate? With regard to music and the arts, we're equal to other nations, as these names will show even over the past hundred years; Byron, Keats, Shelley, Wordsworth, Tennyson, Dickens - oh, I could go on - but you know our emotions are very deep. We enjoy art just as any other nation enjoys it, but we're a shy people and find it difficult to declare our love openly and with loud acclaim. So I hope, with due respect, Signora, you'll understand a little."

Emma's eyes were shining, she had used her hands in expression, and looked a little breathless. Finally, she said, "Forgive me, if you think I've said too much, but I'm British through and through, and just an example, I hope, of my country folk." She turned a little to see Andrew and Lorenzo just inside the door, and was alarmed she had such an audience. Lorenzo came forward and drew Emma to her feet.

"You're quite right to defend what you believe in. Our women folk don't concern themselves so. My family have always been very fortunate, and I doubt very much if my mother gives much thought to the poor around us." His mother came forward and kissed Emma on both cheeks.

"You're very patriotic, my child; it's true what Lorenzo says, I fear I'm far too lazy to bother."

Cristina had been rather amused with the conversation; she was very attached to Emma and hoped her mother-in-law had not upset her with her thoughtless criticism.

Andrew, putting his arm around her shoulder and firmly pressing it said, "Well done, my little Britannia!" and there was much laughter.

At twenty-three Emma had not only developed in looks and decorum, but her imagination, always very vivid, had helped her develop her character too. She found it easy to fit into the society of people around her. She learnt easily, and at times it was even difficult for her to remember from where she had sprung. She had acquired poise and grace. At intervals her mother and Ruth would jog her conscience, and she would write and send a little gift. She had seldom met them since the days of her pregnancy. Andrew, not knowing them, and so never remembering them did not therefore encourage her in her relationship. Emma was so happy that it was now only at odd times that she remembered Diane, and then mostly when she read some society gossip about the Harkness family. Always having Andrew by her side, the fears and nightmares of her earlier life had also sunk into her subconscious.

She was getting used to the knowledge that she might never have another child. Andrew seemed content with her and Carlos. If Henry and his relationship to Carlos gave her cause for thought at times, she was so happy that it could easily be brushed aside. Even his return into her life (temporarily she hoped) had given her no further alarm, now she was out of England. Emma in all her life had never worried too much, and she had a knack of dismissing things, and only really being concerned when confronted. Away from England she managed to push Henry aside; he became a problem to be dealt with later.

Meanwhile, Henry had discovered quite a lot about Emma since she had left England. He was able even to converse with Carlos' Nanny, and when he saw the boy the first time riding his fairy cycle with other children in Hyde Park, while their respective Nannies kept a watchful eye, he knew! He knew that Carlos was his, his flesh and blood, the child of his love and passion for Emma! He was filled with pride as he watched him, then with bitterness at being cheated. A surge of anger arose when he thought of Andrew claiming to be the father, and suddenly a hatred of Emma for what she had done for all three. True, she had told him she did not love him; true, he had said he would be careful and not give her a child. He remembered vividly that last night together, and how he had been determined she would conceive; and, when she discovered this, return to him. Foolishly he had not known that Emma would play a double game. He knew nothing of Andrew, and to have met her and discovered she was married, and had been almost since they had parted, made him bitter. As he stood watching the boy, he promised himself he would get even with the mother. How and when he did not know, but suffer she would, as he had suffered, as he suffered now at hearing Nanny say, "We must go home now, Carlos, because there's a lot to do before we go to Mummy and Dadda."

And Carlos had joyously replied, "I'm so excited, Nanny! Tomorrow they'll be home again. We can say goodbye to Grandma and Gandpapa. Perhaps Dadda will take me riding before I go to my new school? Yes, let's hurry!"

He waved goodbye, and Henry, who was sitting on a nearby seat, almost lost control with the desire to shout, "He is not your father, I am, I am!"

How long he sat, he could not say. Tears of unhappiness gently flowed; he was not ashamed, but bitter.

Chapter Eleven

They had been back from Italy nearly two months. Carlos was now at a preparatory school, and enjoying it. He was a very likeable young fellow, and a good mixer. He had inherited his mother's fine features, beautiful eyes and dark hair. He was growing fairly tall, and was beautifully formed. Once back in England, Emma came face to face with the knowledge that Henry was near at hand. Isobel often came to visit them, but preferred to drive herself. Andrew and Emma had twice been to both lunch and dinner, but Henry was not in sight. Perhaps, said a consoling voice within her, he had left Isobel's employ - it would be unwise to ask, especially after the last time; it might raise a question in Isobel's mind. But no, Henry was near, near enough to keep Emma thinking. He was on holiday and would soon return; George volunteered this little bit of information when he told them, "I'm enjoying myself, with my footman on holiday. Isobel can find no excuse for me not to drive. Dash it all, why shouldn't I? I like a little speed!"

So that was that!

Emma had not told Andrew as yet, but recently she had not been feeling too well. She hoped beyond all else that she was pregnant, and finally she discovered she was. Elated after more than seven years, she hugged her secret for a while, and one night just after the lights were out and they were ready for sleep Emma gave her news to Andrew. So much love and care he showered upon her; he would not leave London to do business; either his brother did the travelling, or else he promoted business over the telephone.

And in August, at their London home, another son was born; a wee mite, fair, delicately featured. They called him John Simon. The world was a happy place for them.

Henry was quietly watching on the horizon; he had seen that a new baby was coming - at best, he kept out of Emma's way. She had ceased some time ago to visit Isobel, and this continued, for the baby filled her daily life. Carlos was almost eight, and it was the year 1933.

With Emma content and his family in good health, Andrew again began to travel for business. His father had recommended a trip to New York, and Emma had agreed that he should go. He would be away for at least six months, and he decided that he would leave directly after Christmas.

At Easter Emma, along with her baby and Nanny, left London to stay for the last three months of Andrew's absence at the little house on the edge of Dartmoor. Carlos was back at his prep school, and her in-laws had returned to London after a swift visit. They hoped she would be content until Andrew returned, but if not, and she felt lonely, they would come immediately and whisk her back to London. But Emma <u>was</u> content. She enjoyed her days with Nanny and John; she enjoyed her brisk walks on the edge of the moors. Andrew had warned her not to go too far in for the mists would rise quickly and suddenly, and she could easily get lost. Up to now no thought of fear of the night, the lonely night, had come to her. She would read in bed for a while, then when she could no longer keep her eyes open, sleep until morning.

At breakfast one morning she received the following letter:

"Dear Emma," it read, "Patiently I have waited. I hope you did not think I had forgotten, as perhaps <u>you</u> may have done. I'm here in Totnes, and at any time after your receiving this I shall call on you. So that you will not wonder when, I can inform you that it will be after the child's nurse has gone to bed, and your daily woman has left for her home. I do not wish to appear melodramatic. I shall come up through the garden and you can let me in. Yours as always, Henry."

So here it was, upon her, and she must now face the consequences.

True to his word, the next night she received a telephone call from him to assure her that within a quarter of an hour he would arrive. He carried a small valise. Quietly he entered and followed her to the drawing room. As quietly he closed the door. Emma turned and looked at him. Tall, dark, handsome, and with something of the look of Carlos. Hardly a day older, and the same flash of broad white teeth that showed as he smiled at her.

"Well, Henry, don't you think this unwise to come here? We have nothing in common now. I'm married with children, and even if I wished to acknowledge that we knew each other in the past, it would be very embarrassing for everyone all around. Our association ended years ago. So why...?" She sank into a chair, and he into another opposite.

"I believe you refuse to face up to things. Let me renew your memory," he mused, stretching his legs and settling himself comfortably. "We were lovers, you know. I loved you, and I still love you. You were an East End kid, ambitious and intending to get on. To marry me would have put a stop to that. You said you were fond of me, but didn't love me. You were an excellent bed partner, and enjoyed my love-making; in fact at times I felt one man was not enough for you. Now don't interrupt," he said, as she seemed about to thrust herself up from the chair and expostulate. "I'm telling you, looking back and thinking of the time when we were lovers - and remember, I've had a long time to think - how I have thought of you! You hurt me when you rejected my offer of marriage, hurt me more than I could tell you even now. I couldn't understand you; when the lights were out and you were in my arms, you were a loving, passionate creature. How I loved you! I was determined to keep you, and so I felt the only way was to give you a child. I could easily have wrung your neck if I'd found you in the early days when you left me so cruelly. That feeling's gone. All I want now is to have you, and claim my son." His voice had trailed off into emotional silence. He took a cigarette from his pocket, lit it and inhaled deeply.

She broke the silence after a while. Her mind was very clear and she made a determined effort to be convincing. "Well, I had no child did I? I met Andrew in Paris, before I went through that awful time, and then we were married soon after I left Cannes. My husband would take this matter up very seriously, Henry, if I were to tell him, but because I know how good and kind you were to me, I won't tell him. Just get out of my life, Henry, and leave me in peace."

"Oh no, old girl, nothing like that! Now, just listen to me some more. Over the past year I've been making plenty of enquiries. I know you lived with your husband in Italy before you were married. I know it's said that Carlos was a premature baby, born seven months after your hasty marriage. I went to visit your sister Ruth, and from her I got the truth. In all innocence she told me. I knew then that I would soon catch up with you. The way I did doesn't matter. I have seen my son. I know beyond doubt he's mine. I've talked to his Nanny. I'm familiar with everything. Now, admit to me, Emma, that the boy is ours."

Tears filled Emma's eyes. She had no defences. Falteringly she asked, "If I admit what you've just said to me is true, what will you do? I'm married, happily, and we love each other very much. Andrew loves both our boys very much and is proud of them."

"Yes. Maybe that's so, but don't try to tell me that he believes Carlos is his. Surely the man is not so dense as to recognise a full term child from a premature one, and even if he was, there would have been sufficient medical attention to convince him one way or the other. Anyway, I'm not asking. I really don't want to know. The information I got from Ruth is all I need."

In desperation, and rising to her feet, Emma said, "All right, Henry, supposing what you say is true, and I only say supposing, tell me what you want. Not Carlos, surely?"

"No! Not Carlos. You, Emma, just you!" drawing her towards him, he held her across his legs, bringing her body close to him. "Just you, Emma. Whenever I want you, you must come to me, or I to you." Kissing her throat, she trying to struggle up, Henry said "Keep still, my darling, and listen to me. Tonight I stay. I'll leave early in the morning. While your husband's away I'll take his place, or rather, I'll resume where I left off, before he took over. We'll keep this secret. I shall enjoy the difficulties you get into, and have to wriggle out of. We'll make love as we used to, and you will enjoy it, because although I love you, I know at heart you're a little harlot. So come." Still holding one arm as he pushed her to her feet, he rose. "I have my overnight things here," he said, indicating his valise. "Come, there's a lot overdue."

And with the morning there was no remorse. Henry had gone quietly, and she was aware that this was to be continued. Loving Andrew as she did, she reflected that the needs of the body for her were quite separate. The darkness of the night had obliterated all sense of decency and loyalty, and once awakened by Henry's love-making, all else had been forgotten. As time passed she was often disgusted with herself, and often nervous as to the outcome.

Andrew eventually returned from America, elated with his business success and the joy of seeing his family once again. Emma went to him physically and sexually as easily as ever. As was usual with her, she brushed aside the future, and lived in her own paradise day by day.

Back in London Henry soon made her aware that he no longer worked for Isobel and George Kemp. He was head waiter at the Cafe Royal, and had taken a flat right at the top of a converted Kensington mansion, in a secluded spot off Sloane Square. The only entry was by lift which he said, would be very suitable when she visited him. He was very understanding about the fact that at times she would be out of London, but when not, it was decided that she would visit him once a week. Wednesday afternoon was agreed upon, because Andrew never came home early that day, always calling on his parents for cocktails. And now that all these arrangements seemed to dovetail, Andrew was save about knowing about Henry, and Carlos kept from being taken from Emma. She seemed to lose all fear of discovery, and began to look eagerly towards the Wednesday rendezvous. She regained much of her former affection for Henry; she responded to his love-making in no small measure.

But Henry was under no illusion. He loved her as before, as he always would. But she was a baggage and selfish, she was greedy for him and love! But love him as he wished, she never would. So he took what he could, when he could, and shut his mind to Andrew altogether. Emma had thought it prudent to admit that Carlos was Henry's. He had made little comment, satisfied now that he had her admission. His dream of Emma as a wife, and their children around them, had faded long ago. He was interested in the boy, and had even extracted a photo of Carlos which stood on his desk. Emma thought that no harm could come by giving him it, as no one that she knew would ever visit Henry's flat.

When Carlos was twelve and Simon four, Andrew's father died. He had been ill for quite a while; suddenly he had a severe heart attack, and the result was final. It was a terrible shock to Lady Craig, and she became very difficult for both of her sons to cope with until a distant cousin, living in San Diego, suggested she go out to live with her for an indefinite time. Her family were relieved that she had accepted, and Andrew arranged to take her and, at the same time, attend to business in America and France on the way home. But he would not leave without Emma. She had protested, because she wouldn't leave without the children. Carlos, said Andrew, would be quite all right. He was now at public school and Isobel would, he felt sure, have him for holidays. Simon, he said, could come with them though it would be difficult travelling with Lady Craig, who continued to take the loss of Andrew's father very badly. Simon's Nanny would also be going, and would look after Simon, mostly taking him off their hands.

So seldom did Emma's mother and sister enter her mind that when Andrew suggested that she visit them before leaving, she was surprised. Yet she went, and was received by Ruth very coolly at first. Emma was never one to boast. Ruth had read of her father-in-law's death, and that Andrew would now succeed him as head of a vast wine empire. There was also a knighthood and the country mansion in Dorset, a shoot in Scotland, and a small house in Half Moon Street. Emma had travelled down to Canning Town by train and bus. She was thoughtful and didn't wish to embarrass either Ruth or herself by arriving in a chauffeur-driven car. Their mother had been widowed for some time, and was living with Ruth. She did not welcome Emma too kindly.

"I wonder you have the neck to come here! I suppose it's only to show off, now you have a title since the old man died!" she said sharply and without any preludes. "Where's them grandchildren of mine? I suppose we're not good enough? Don't stand there staring, for goodness sake. Sit down! Make the young lady a cup of tea. I can do with one myself. A pity you don't do something to help us, with all those fine clothes, and things - but there!" Words were falling short, her temper pushing all else out. She snuggled back into her wooden armchair, adjusted her glasses, and studiously settled into her newspaper, boiling with rage, a rage which had always swamped any commonsense she may have had. And then, quite suddenly, she looked up again. "Yes, I'm having another good look at you, my lady, and I can see her, yes, there she is, right in you, your dirty whoring mother!"

"Be quiet, can't you!" Ruth said. "Keep your mouth closed if you can't say anything pleasant. Emma stays away because this is what she always gets, except the last bit. She has a right to live where she likes, and do as she pleases. She has a good husband, and we should be pleased about it all. I'll make a good cup of tea, Emms, and then we can have a talk."

"Well, you can bring mine to my room. I don't think I can drink in such fine company!" And their mother stormed out of the room.

All this time Emma had remained silent. Past experience had come to her aid, and she knew that silence was the better part of valour. Their mother had often been goaded into striking them if they gave what she called "back answers".

Now, drinking her tea, Emma enquired, "What did she mean, when she referred to 'my mother'? Isn't she my mother?"

Ruth remained silent for a while, and thoughtfully stirred her tea. "Take a biscuit, Emms, and have you got enough sugar?" she enquired.

"Now, don't sidetrack, Ruth; tell me what I want to know. What was the meaning of this outburst? Tell me!"

"Oh, well, you've a right to know. You don't belong to us; for that matter, none of us belongs to each other. Mother married my father, who was widowed, and he already had Jimmy and me. Jim was eleven, and I was nine. From the first she hated me, and idolised Jim. But Jim, when he was old enough, left home, and shared a flat with friends until he married.

"My life was really miserable. I missed Jim, and so did mother, who seemed to be more cruel to me than ever. When I was twenty, she was asked to nurse a young unmarried girl with her first baby. That was you, but it turned out that you weren't the first; she already had a little girl of two, called Connie. Your natural mother said she couldn't keep you, and if someone couldn't help her she'd kill you by `accidentally' lying on you. Our mother told this story to our father, who had a large and gentle heart. Even little birds would stay quiet in his large hands. Straight away he said to bring you home, and she did, because she was, and still is, very impetuous, but very quickly does all she can to push away the responsibility that comes with impulses.

"At the time you were the impulse, pushed quickly on to me, and I welcomed you as someone to love and care for. All my leisure time was spent with you. Then one day I met Tom. She did everything possible to stop our courting and wherever we were, wherever we went you had to be with us. Quite late at night she would come home, drunk and abusive, hurling things at both Tom and me. She would pawn my Sunday clothes so that I had to stay home; she would make me stand at the wash tub till midnight to finish clothes she should have done instead of spending hours over the garden fence with her cronies.

"Tom had told his parents about what I had to go through. They were quiet people, and very kind to me. Tom persuaded me to leave home, and live with them until we married. I left like a thief in the night. She was mad, I heard. I had to change my job at Clarnico's factory to Slazengers, where we made tennis balls, because she'd stand at the gate of the factory with you in her arms, telling everyone who knew me that you were my child.

"Then my father died of a stroke, quite suddenly, and I, wanting a truce between us, went home for the funeral. It was there I met your mother. Apparently she had been asked what she was going to do about you. The answer - nothing. She had married, married well, and didn't intend to take you into her family circle. Connie, whom she adored, she'd always kept. I can see her now, tall, fair, and very lovely. She fascinated me. You're like her in many ways. You have her smile, her beautiful mouth, but otherwise you must have been like your father. I found she lived in Hampstead, and after I was married I used to go and see her. Her husband was older than her, and had a grown family. But all the time I knew her she would never discuss having you to live with her. She said her husband had accepted Connie, but she would never had stood a chance with you as well.

“One day when I called, I was a little earlier than usual. I climbed the steps to the front door which was already open, and a man whom I saw later was tall and dark, was just leaving. Maud, your mother, looked annoyed when she first saw me, but quickly had got over whatever she may have felt about my early visit.

“Well, to make the story short, I soon discovered that this man was her lover, had been since before you were born. He wasn’t Connie’s father. Who he was, I don’t know. As for you, he knew nothing about you, you had been and, as far as she could possibly help, would remain a secret. He was married and was head of a large tobacco firm. She had been in his employ as a cigar maker. As I said before, she had a way with her, and he fell hard. She did too, and although she’d married, it had only been in case of any more children, whom she intended to foster on her husband.

“During the many times I went to see her I got to know such a lot about her, and once she felt confident that I could keep my mouth shut, she confided in me. She was a fascinating woman. I became very attached to her. Then, quite suddenly she disappeared - where, with whom, her husband never knew. But I did, I knew as though she’d told me. Her love for your father, and his for her, was too much and they had gone away together.

About a year later I read about a well-known businessman who had left England some time ago, and had sold through his solicitors his business, and settled a large sum of money on his childless wife. And then, of course, I knew who your father was. I kept away from my stepmother in case I ever divulged anything. I knew about your parents.

But the urge to see you often came on me until at last I gave in, and you can remember I came to see you. I’ve said quite a lot, for me. I don’t remember ever saying so much before. I want you always to think about her, to remember her. Maud was a lovable, fascinating woman. I’m sorry she never wanted you. I know the feeling. But she loved your father as he loved her. It’s hard to understand.”

Emma sat very quietly listening and thinking. So she was a bastard! She belonged to no one. Even the woman she thought of as a mother and Ruth, were not hers. She had not thought of them seriously for years. Very occasionally she would write, perhaps send a little gift, and then forget about them. But not to belong at all was a shock. A sense of hatred welled up within her towards the woman who had given birth to her, to the sister who had been wanted and therefore loved. Why had she been cheated? Cheated! But that was what she too had done. Cheated Andrew of his rightful heir, cheated Carlos of his natural father, cheated Simon of his inheritance. Oh, it was laughable, she thought bitterly; here she was, judging Maud, when she herself had done, if not exactly, very much the same towards her own child. Yet she hadn't pushed him aside, as she had been pushed aside. Oh, no!...Keeping him and loving him had come afterwards. She had tried to murder him mentally, and had almost succeeded. Maud, no doubt had done the same, perhaps the gin, the hot baths, even worse. Emma shuddered. Life was a circle, history repeating itself.

"You're very quiet, Emma. I hope you're not upset. Mother should have told you years ago. She's old now, and her mind gets very mixed up. I'm sure if it wasn't you would never have heard any of this. Try to think kindly of her. Like me, she's quite ignorant; but we try to do our best despite our many faults."

Emma was still silent; she was gazing at the rug, but did not see it. Instead, she saw herself being presented at Court, as she would be in six months time. Isobel was launching her. Andrew thought she should. Cheating again. She should be introduced as what she really was, a bastard, a woman who had fostered another man's child on to her husband, and in order to keep from him the knowledge of the child's true father, was blackmailed into committing adultery at regular intervals. But no; blackmailed at first, but now accepting it and, admit it, Emma, enjoying it. She was corrupt, full of sex, full of the base enjoyment of the sensual practices of the flesh. She castigated herself; she was self-indulgent, carnal, licentious, gratifying the flesh, stimulating the aesthetic senses. All inherited, she could see.

Drawing herself together she replied to Ruth, "Oh, don't worry, Ruth. It's long past. I'm happily married, and where I came from has never bothered Andrew. Our children are being reared as children should be in our position. They're very happy children. I hope what I'm about to say won't hurt you or be misunderstood. It'll be best for all of us if I don't come here again. I only upset your home, as I have today, and take back with me unhappy thoughts. It's best for the children too, never to know about my birth." She rose from her chair and was about to gather up her bag, but Ruth was quicker, and pushed her gently back, saying, with a hint of a temper: "Oh no, you don't go so quickly! I could've agreed at one time that you were better away from us for good. Your ways were always uppish to ours, but that I tried to understand. But now you say you'll stay away, because we're not good enough. Oh, all right," she conceded as Emma protested, "not in so many words, but you meant it just the same. Well, stay away, do as you like, only always remember I know everything, yes, everything! Shall I remind you? Not only is the first boy Henry's, which you admitted years ago to me; but for a long time you've carried on an affair with Henry - don't interrupt, I know it all, Henry's told me. I even know which days you go - Henry doesn't brag about it, but you've made him suffer so much. God knows why he's kept so quiet; I suppose it's some misguided love he has for you. Yes, you can go now, but one last thing before you do; when you think of Maud, and you will, remember what I tell you, Emms; you're two peas in the same pod; men fall for you; you like it. You have more than your share of sex, and so had she!"

The East End kid in Emma rose swiftly to the surface. "Shut up! Shut up! I can't help the way I'm made. You're jealous, yes, jealous! Thank goodness I got the chance to better myself, even if I <u>did</u> have to lie on my back to get it. Yes, Ruth, you're jealous and dried up." She rushed into the little passage and, opening the street door, hastily took to her heels.

The only mother she had ever known opened her bedroom door and called, "Has Emma gone? She rushed out without saying ta ta!"

It was natural for Emma to push anything unpleasant in her life to the back of her mind. Her illegitimacy, once she had got over the first shock, she endeavoured to forget. She had status now;

Andrew loved and trusted her; she had, of course, destroyed that trust time and time again, betrayed it. She wouldn't tell him what she had now discovered about herself, no more than she would ever tell him about Henry. She was capable of clever strategy, and this she pursued. If her conscience at any time troubled her, she told herself that she was quite willing to suffer, but shield Andrew and Carlos she must. She fancied herself as a martyr, protecting her family from her earlier indiscretions. And now she had to tell Henry that she would be away for quite a time. He wouldn't like her absence to be too prolonged, and she would have to pacify him with some sort of tale about returning as soon as possible.

Chapter Twelve

They spent two years in America. Emma enjoyed every moment of it. Simon was now a boy of nine. Unlike his brother, he was slight and fair, with delicate features. He had inherited the large brown eyes of his mother, otherwise he was certainly a Craig. He was shy, nervous, inquisitive, but beneath the delicate exterior he had a will of iron, matched easily with a terrific temper when things didn't go his way. For one so young he showed signs of a haughty temperament. His father engaged a tutor, as he was timid to join boys of his own age at a public school. Carlos had been brought over to America in the second year, and was now a day pupil at a nearby college. The brothers had a very close attachment to each other. Emma, conscious of the difference of their birth, did all she could to keep them together, to encourage them to love each other.

But this she need not concern herself about. Carlos loved Simon from the moment he was born. He was protective, and always kind. He enjoyed the love that Simon returned, and despite the difference in age, they had much in common. Simon looked up to Carlos, so tall, dark and handsome. He loved to join him in games; he loved animals because Carlos loved them; he learned to love them for themselves later. And they also had in common a deep, very deep love for their mother. They loved their father, but at times he was rather shadowy. But their mother - well, she gathered them close to her, with her smile, her singing voice, her enveloping love. If their father entered a room where their mother was already, he would see <u>her</u> first, kiss <u>her</u> first, and after a while turn to them, perhaps saying, "How are you both, my boys? I hope you've been quite good." But mother always saw them first, her arms would envelop them, and she would have no time for anyone else. They spent a great deal of time with her..

Cristina and Lorenzo Ferraris had been in New York for six months. Both their daughters had married Americans, and they had just visited them. Now they came to San Diego to pay a short visit to Emma and Andrew. It was 1938, late summer. Suspense was mounting in the world as Britain and France made a stand against the German dictator.

What will you do, Andrew, if this disturbing news in Europe continues?" asked Lorenzo as the four of them sat on a patio in the falling summer dusk. "Will you go back to England with your family, or will you remain here?"

"As a matter of fact, we haven't given the matter serious thought, but I suppose if trouble does arise, we'll return home as soon as possible. What are you both doing?"

"We're considering staying here in America. Our daughters are now American citizens; we don't want to live in Italy now, under Mussolini's regime. Here we're far from it all. Some years ago we arranged for most of our capital to be deposited in Switzerland, so we've no financial difficulties. England is none too friendly with Italy over Ethiopia, but I'm sure America will keep out of Europe's quarrels." Turning to Cristina, Lorenzo continued, "This is the better course, cara mia, and one day all will be peaceful, and we'll return to our beloved country. Meanwhile, it's better that we remain here."

"Tell me, Andrew, because I haven't paid much attention to news in Europe, are things very bad at home?" asked Emma.

"Well, Nazi Germany has growing power, Baby. Our prime minister, Neville Chamberlain, has met Hitler and in my opinion the peril of war has only been temporarily averted. They both signed an agreement that their countries wouldn't go to war against each other again. Personally, I can't quite take that in. Czechoslovakia is already being sacrificed, Winston Churchill had asked for a recall of Parliament, and has made some very sweeping observations about what might happen."

"Do you mean to tell me that our country may go to war, Andrew? Surely, after the last war, which was to end all wars, no one in his right mind can think of it." Emma looked concerned.

"As you say, 'no one in his right mind', but is the German government in its right senses? Hitler is a fanatic and his followers equally so. I foresee war in the future. As far as I can tell, it's impossible for the British government to have a friendly relationship with a Nazi Germany."

"Oh dear, what shall we do? Should we go home, or should we stay here? There are the boys to consider, and your mother."

"Well, let's not jump our fences before we arrive at them. Don't worry, let's go in and play a hand of cards."

But worry they had to in a very short time. The radio and press began to broadcast alarming news. Children in England were to be evacuated. Some were coming to America. There was conscription in Britain. In April 1939, Mussolini took Albania, and then Poland fell to Germany. There was no alternative; on September 3rd Great Britain and France declared war on Germany. At 11.00 am, as the prime minister was telling the nation on the radio that war had been declared, the first of many hundreds of sirens was sounded, and the people of Great Britain took cover.

There was great consternation in the hearts of both Emma and Andrew. They decided to return at once to England. Andrew's mother, Cristina and Lorenzo all wanted to keep the boys, but Carlos himself settled what should be done with them.

"Mother, you can't leave us behind! We're British and none of us can shirk our duties. Simon would die if you left him here - mother, you know how timid he is! Please tell father not to leave us here. Please, mother!"

"But I could stay here with you, darling. The war won't last for long, and then we can all be together again." She was always pushing unpleasant things aside.

"Mother, don't talk like this. You know that you and father hate to be separated. Besides, I want to go home. I want to be there when all this is happening!"

"So do I, so do I, mummy!" said Simon. "I want to see it all with Carlos." He flung his arms around her waist. "Please, ask Dadda to take us all home!"

She laughed happily; she felt no fear of what might happen, only joy that her sons were with her, and wished to be with her. "I'll talk to your father, but if he says we must stay in America, we'll have to."

And so in October they all sailed for England in an American liner. The crossing was fraught with danger and horror. The

Germans had inflicted outrage upon outrage on their enemy by their U-boat campaigns and their indiscriminate bombing. Many times did Andrew wish he had left them back in America. Many times during the voyage did Emma pray for forgiveness for not being firm with her own emotions and leaving her beloved children in safety. But God protected them, and eventually they docked, after some very brilliant seamanship which avoided the magnetic mines scattered heedlessly from the air by the enemy around the coastal waters.

The sirens wailed their terrifying warning as the family's feet touched English soil. Carlos was excited and gripped his father's arm. He would have remained to see the air warfare, but they were all hastily conducted to a shelter, and there they experienced their first air raid, one of very many they were to live through.

Andrew took them to the little house in Devon, hoping that they would settle there. He immediately responded to his call-up papers, but his medical showed that he had a disorder of the liver, and he was suspended for six months. Restless to be taking an active part in the war, as his brother was already doing, Andrew left his firm (which during the war years was to diminish to a great extent) in the capable hands of men who had retired in his father's time from the Board of Directors and were now willing to resume their responsibility. He quickly manoeuvered things and acquired a post in the Intelligence Department. He was fluent in several languages, and had made many connections in Europe and America which were to prove useful to this particular department. He arranged for Carlos to enter the evacuated school of Westminster. Carlos was nearly fifteen, tall beyond his age and almost on a level with Andrew's six feet. He was extremely well proportioned, and had grown into a handsome youth. Simon, still a nervous child, and needing his mother so much, would be a day pupil at the local grammar school.

"But, darling," said Emma amid all the preparations, "I can't stay here without you - I'll go mad with nothing to do. I'm coming back to London with you!"

"You must stay here, Baby. I'll be going away more often than I'll ever be with you, and London is not the place for you to be. Simon needs you, and I won't permit my son to be in such danger when it's not necessary." His voice was quite sharp, and it struck Emma that he had put special emphasis on the words " my son". A wave of sickness enveloped her. After all these years, he still remembered; there it was, right in front of his nose!

"Andrew! Do you know what you've just said? You've just told me that you remember. You remember quite clearly about Carlos. All these years, you've kept it alive." She was raising her voice, and he closed the drawing room door for fear the boys might hear their voices.

"Be quiet, Emma, I don't want to talk about it. If I said a word, or change a tone, anything that upset you, I'm sorry. Carlos is my son just as Simon's my son. I love them equally. Please dismiss anything else from your mind." But it didn't leave her mind any more than it left Andrew's.

The family solicitor came down for a weekend, and was for quite a time closeted with Andrew in his little study. When he left on the early Monday train, Emma could not stand the gnawing anxiety longer, and promptly came to the point when the boys left to shop in the village.

"I know Mr Drake has been instructed to make a new will for you. Tell me, darling, where does Carlos come into this?" She was fidgeting with a paper knife on his desk, and her eyes were lowered. Her heart was leaping, and a heavy pulse beat in her throat.

There was silence for a few moments, then Andrew came round the desk, and lifted her up in his arms.

"My sweet, don't be so agitated!" he said in a soothing voice, "I assure you, both boys are treated equally. If I die before you, you're to be the chief beneficiary and legal guardian of my sons. Hush!" He continued as she was about to interrupt, "I know you so well, my love, and so before the question's asked, Carlos' birth remains a secret. He's my heir, and will be the future baronet."

"But Simon should be; <u>he's</u> your heir. Andrew, Andrew, what have I done? Cheated everyone, even our little Simon!" She was getting very excited.

"Now, don't be so melodramatic, Emma. If you want to rake all this up, remember I agreed to accept Carlos as my son. It's a long time ago - perhaps I did sire him. Oh Hell, why rake all this up? The war is enough to break up families; don't let's help by whys and wherefores. We'll be separated often - the boys in one place, you perhaps in another, and I, God knows where. We've had a very happy life - I love you today as I did in the beginning." And pulling her close to him he said, "My darling, how shall we live apart? It's unthinkable!" His voice was shaky; he kissed her long and deep. Suddenly the boys burst into the room.

Carlos cried, "She's a lovely mother!" and hugged the two of them, while Simon fell to his knees, trying to clasp her legs.

And so Andrew went away to his job in the Intelligence Corps, Carlos to his school, and Simon stayed as a border at the grammar school. Emma returned to London, very much against Andrew's wishes. But she was energetic, wanted to be of use and he understood. She took two rooms in a small hotel in Sloane Street, which was quite enough, and didn't bother to try to get domestic help. Then she took a post with the Auxilliary Nursing Service, and felt she was really doing something. On leave days she either visited Carlos or Simon, on odd occasions with Andrew. But his comings and goings were very vague, and sometimes he would be away for a couple of months at a time.

Then into her life once again came Henry, in full splendour, in the uniform of an officer of the Merchant Navy. He had been called up almost as soon as hostilities had commenced, because of his previous record. He was stationed at the East India Docks, and seemed to enjoy it.

"How did you know where to find me after being away so long?" she asked in amazement, when he had enquired for her at the hospital as she came off duty.

"Ems, my dear," he said, as without more ado he enveloped her within his large embrace, and kissed her fully on the mouth, much to her consternation, as people were passing to and fro. "Ems, my darling, I've known every move you've made since you left England. It has cost me a pretty penny, but I'm still interested in my son, you know - and you!"

"Oh, hush!" She drew him into the blacked-out street. "I thought that was all past! Why don't you leave me alone? Anyway, we can't stand talking here. Where shall we go?"

Taking her by the elbow, he smiled, "You look good in your uniform. Where shall we go? To my flat, which I've kept on, and which is near your hotel. Come, I've got a taxi waiting."

They became lovers again. He told her there had never been anyone else since she had gone away. He would hold her tightly in his arms, demanding; she would give, and in the morning hate herself. He would be away for long lengths of time, as Andrew was, but when he could be he would be back again, waiting at the hospital. On one occasion Andrew was there, and Henry had to return to his flat alone, seething within himself, imagining the two together.

Before long they were again at his flat. Emma was hoping to end it, he was in a flurry of kisses, anticipating future clandestine meetings. With the many promises she made him, she was conscious that she was a traitor. She lay in Andrew's arms and revelled in the warmth of his love. He was innocent of her affair with Henry. But Henry and Emma knew each other, understood each other, and even enjoyed each other.

As time went on, amid the lightheartedness that war inevitably brings, that feeling of 'here today, gone tomorrow', Emma stifled all her sense of right and wrong. She made up her mind that her sacrifice, if she could call it such, was well worth while. Andrew was blissfully ignorant of Henry; Carlos was secure; Henry had her body if not her love. But the truth of the whole matter was that gradually Emma began to enjoy it all - the "sacrifice", keeping the two men apart, both loving her, both excellent bedfellows, and she thrived.

The Battle of Britain was at its peak. Death was ever-present. Andrew had been gone some time. The hospital was full of casualties - London was heroically taking a severe beating. Squadron after squadron of the Luftwaffe rained down their bombs on London and the dock-side. The gallant Royal Air Force, outnumbered, fought valiantly in the skies, and put the enemy to flight. The men and women below were working hard to save the towns and villages.

Henry came to Emma amidst all this, tired, red-eyed and silent. His love-making was a ferocious attempt to wipe out the horror he had experienced. He should not have been away from duty; but his heart and mind had yearned so much for her that he had got away early one evening. How he had travelled through the raids he didn't know, and didn't care. He had tried to wipe out the horror with Emma in his arms, and she, with a love that was born of sympathy, had given herself to him in the way he had always wanted. He had cried when dawn broke, when sirens again rang out, and she had soothed him, "Hush, Henry, I can't bear to hear you so. Hush, my love!"

"Emma," he said, clinging like a child to her, "Emma, I won't come back; I feel it. I love you, darling. I can't bear to go. Let me hear you say you love me - let me hear it, Emma, as though you're my wife! You're the mother of my son - oh, say you love me!"

She looked at him, a great big man, always kind and loving to her, and loyal. What did it matter if it made him happy, to say the words he wanted to hear? The fever of hope lay deep in his eyes, and they brightened with certainty as she said, "I love you, Henry, love you! I can't do otherwise; hold me close, my love, all will be well. Don't distress yourself. I love you, perhaps I always have." May God forgive me, she thought as she continued, "And to show you it's true I want you to take me again; love me as you never have before!"

Hungrily he kissed her. "Oh, God, if it were true, I'd die happy, for I won't come back, but I'll leave my heart with you. All the beautiful things in this world will tell you of my love, and when the flowers bloom, the birds sing, they'll be a reminder of my heart that beats for you, wherever it may be. Roses I would shower on you, and put across your path, white and pink and yellow, and in this beautiful hair, red roses, and near your heart, red roses - red roses for love!"

They lay together until early noon. He left her to return to duty; she went to the hospital. A few days later a letter came from him.

"My darling,

This is goodbye! I've been posted - naturally I can't

tell you more, nor can I write much more. Thank you for the beautiful lie, that you love me; I know your heart was given years ago. Yet the lie was just the thing to raise my spirits. Remember me in my son, Carlos - he will, of course, never know me. And be careful, my darling, of the last time we were together - our emotions ran high. God bless and protect you both,

Henry."

She did not see Henry again. Later she heard from Ruth how he had died. In a short while Henry's warning came true. Once again she was pregnant - once again Henry's child was fostered on Andrew, her beloved.

Chapter Thirteen

The bombing of London and all the main towns of England, on and around the coast, continued. Andrew came home on fleeting leave, and the time they spent with each other was satisfying to Andrew, agonising to Emma. She was torn into so many pieces. Andrew's missions were secret; he could tell her nothing, and he looked to her for comfort in every way. They went together to visit the boys. Carlos was becoming restless, and begged to leave school and play a small part in the strife. Andrew remarked that it was utter nonsense in one so young, and he must be content to remain and work hard at school.

"But, father!" Carlos protested on one of these occasions, "I'm so tall, I weigh twelve stone, everybody in my form is small. I feel years ahead of them. Let me try to get a job in a munitions factory. I'd at least be doing something, and when the war's over, I'll go back to my studies."

"Neither your mother nor I will hear of it, son," Andrew said, putting a steady hand on Carlos' shoulder. "I can imagine how you fell, patriotic, God save the King and all that, but it won't do. Be content, it'll be soon over."

But Carlos was not to accept such light treatment. He shrugged his father's hand from his shoulder, and with angry eyes said to both of them, "I'll find a way to do something! Don't you both realise I'm older than my years? Can't you both see how serious I am? This feeling inside me, this urge to do something active is very definite. I no longer think as a boy - I feel as a man!"

Emma, more than Andrew, was disturbed. She knew Carlos much better than Andrew; he was so much like herself. She also knew Simon so much more. Andrew she loved, she loved her children too - but Andrew could only love her, she was first in his thoughts, in his plans; the children he was simply fond of. Of course, when she analysed this, Andrew's feelings could have sprung subconsciously from his knowledge of Carlos' origins. He may have restrained himself from showering too much love on Simon, because the natural springs of love could not possibly flow towards Carlos. These things she only surmised, but she was confident that she was right.

And now, having been assured by her doctor that she was to have another child, this time no thought of what she should do entered her mind. She accepted it, Andrew accepted it, saying it was unfortunate that now he would be away, she must go through it alone. The Cockney kid that was the real Emma took it all philosophically. She left London, returned to Dartmoor, had Simon brought home, and took in a local woman for help. She had received a letter from Ruth telling her that their mother had been evacuated to Suffolk; she and Tom were homeless. Ruth was living with other families in a school. Tom, because of his work in the docks, was stationed there and not permitted to leave. Ruth came to Emma's cottage and they tried to live quietly together and wait for the new baby. Emma prayed for a daughter. Ruth knitted happily for its arrival. They felt isolated but the radio gave them any immediate news the government felt obliged to release. Quentin Reynolds and Priestley were giving weekly talks to counteract the poisonous venom that the traitor Joyce, otherwise known at the time as Lord Haw Haw, was relaying from Germany. Duff Cooper and Anthony Eden were doing their utmost to encourage, through the medium of radio the people of Britain to go forward and endure. Hearts were beating fast, emotions running high. Anthony Eden, quoting from Richard II, said,

"This Royal Throne of Kings, this sceptred isle,
This earth of Majesty, this seat of Mars,
This other Eden, demi paradise,
This fortress built by Nature for herself
Against infection and the hand of war
This happy breed of men, this little world,
This precious stone, set in a silver sea,
Which serves it in the office of a wall,
Or, as a moat, defensive to a house
Against the envy of less happy lands,
This blessed plot, this earth, this realm, this England."

On hearing it, Emma almost burst with patriotism.

And then came the appeal to the young men of eighteen to volunteer for the army with the assurance that if the war should last, at the most, for two years, they would not be drafted overseas. Carlos heard this, and acted promptly. With permission to visit his mother, he immediately travelled to London, recruited, and was enlisted in the Royal Army Service Corps without any questions asked. He was told to report to a unit in Southend-on-Sea the next day. He travelled home and gave his news to Emma.

She was aghast, speechless. Ruth commented that everyone was doing it. The room was very quiet after Carlos had delivered his bombshell. For a while Emma remained motionless, silent. Andrew was far away - where she did not know. This was something she was confronted with, and had to deal with alone. She looked at Carlos, tall, upright, broad of shoulder, looking down at her with the eyes of a very determined young man. He was no longer a child, but was advanced beyond his years, as she had always been. She saw in him a shadow of herself.

"Darling," she said at last, appealingly, for this was the only way she knew to deal with the situation. "Darling, I know how you feel, everyone wanting to do his bit, and how romantic it appears to young boys like you! But don't think I or your father will permit this. I'll go with you tomorrow and tell the authorities how you are lying about your age. Anyway, you aren't fifteen yet! Ridiculous! You need a spanking, really you do, upsetting me like this!" She was beginning to feel sorry for herself. She was without Andrew; she was pregnant. Ruth was company, but she had her worries too, so Emma couldn't get much comfort from her. Little did she know, her comments made Carlos' resolve firmer than ever. His mouth had a determined set, his eyes, which always shone with ready laughter, looked down at her with hard intent.

"Mother, please listen to me, and try to understand. Every day we either hear or read that we're all in this war together, every man, woman and child. If you stop me, if father stops me, I'll find some other way to join the forces. The country's desperate for men, I feel like a man, and if you try to stop me, I'll enlist under another name. No questions are asked, no birth certificates demanded. Any one of us could be killed any time or place, and if I'm to die in this war, let me die in uniform, serving our country, not in an air raid shelter. I know, mother, how you must feel." He drew her to him and gave her one of his lovely smiles. "I'm sorry to distress you, but try to understand me. I need to go with your love and approval, not to run off and disappear from you." He kissed her. Tears were not far away from either of them. Ruth sat and watched silently. This was not her affair, and she must let it run its course.

"Besides, mother," Carlos valiantly offered a little balm, "the war will be over before two years are up, and I've been assured that youths who join at eighteen won't be drafted overseas."

"You are fifteen, not eighteen!" Emma wanted to call out, but instead she quietly said, "I do know, my Carlos, how you feel. There aren't many years between us. I too am impulsive. If you think this is the right thing, then you must do it but, darling, I can't say yes, only that I hope by morning you'll have changed your mind."

Later, when it was near bed time and Carlos had already gone, Ruth consolingly told Emma that every cloud has its silver lining, and she felt all would be well. "Things seem to be that way for you, Emma. Just look back. How you left home, the awful time in Paris, Henry, and how you shoved him off. Then you married Andrew, and Henry lost his son to someone else. But you'll see, everything'll come right. I've known all along that you and Henry continued to be lovers, and you've never been caught. You won't now - poor Henry!"

Startled, Emma exclaimed, "What do you mean - won't now? What do you know?"

"Well, sometime or other I'd have to tell you, so why not now, Emms? Just before I came down here I received official notice. Henry had given my name as the person to be notified in case he was killed or wounded. There was a terrible bombardment at sea, and Henry died!"

Speechless, Emma sat there. Her heart bled for him, for the man from whom she had accepted so much goodness, and to whom she had caused so much pain. For his love, his loyalty, his loneliness, his unhappiness. The time was gone for making amends. He had loved her unselfishly; she had cheated him of his son; she had cheated him of happiness. Andrew had thought he had stood by her in the early days of their marriage, when all the time there was Henry just waiting to marry her, who had deliberately given her a child, hoping she would return to him. She put out a hand and placed it on Ruth's arm, and then, without looking at her, she left the room and went up to Carlos, who was already in bed. He smiled; did she fancy she saw Henry? She could say no word, but gathered him into her arms - her son, her first-born. Her tears mingled with his. No words were said, they kissed and she left the room. The next morning Carlos left for his depot; she watched him swinging down the road, whistling, while his little dog, Judy, whined in Emma's arms. He disappeared from sight. The baby stirred within her.

Time passed rather slowly. Andrew had shown a great deal of anger about Carlos. Emma had done her best and succeeded in persuading him to let Carlos have his way. She fretted a great deal because of her inactivity, and longed to take part herself. There was so much time to think. Henry's pressure haunted her, it seems she, from earlier tests, knows it is definitely Henry's baby. She read, she sewed, she wrote letters to all her friends. She was restless, and remained so throughout her pregnancy. Andrew had told Carlos' headmaster that he had decided to take his son away from school, and as Carlos had reached leaving age, there was no difficulty.

"I can't deny, Sir Andrew," said the Head during the interview, "that this is the right course. Carlos has been most restless and inattentive. I've had occasion to listen to the housemaster about the unsettled state that the young fellow was in. His recent medical report is here," he added, proferring it to Andrew. "You can read what our doctor has to say."

Andrew took it and thoughtfully read it. Glancing up and looking the Head fully in the eye, he said, "I see here that Carlos has developed years ahead of his age, both physically and mentally. He weighs thirteen stone, is six feet one tall, in perfect health, and except for an operation for appendicitis, has never been ill. Well, headmaster, to have a son so sound in wind and limb is something to be proud of - yes, I think he's better away from school, especially now. Thank you for understanding. His mother will be proud of him too. I'm sure," he said, rising and offering a hand, "this war is taking its toll, and one feels at times dispirited when the young go so willingly to give their lives."

"It's certainly the case. I wish you all God speed, and may I offer you my sincere condolences at the loss of your brother. So many of my former pupils have already lost their lives. The school remembers them daily, and those taking active part just now. Carlos, I'm sure, will succeed in filling a niche, and we'll all be very proud of him."

And so the interview ended, and Andrew later told Emma that he felt sure the Head had suspected the true reason for Carlos' leaving school, and also that he understood, even if perhaps he didn't agree.

Then the day came when Andrew told Emma he had been drafted overseas. Later he wrote that he was somewhere in the Middle East.

"I've only got three days with you, darling, and then God knows when we meet again," he said as they strolled in the garden after dinner. "I feel so awful when I think of you having the baby alone. But Ruth is with you, and that's a small comfort; she'll take care of you all. Tomorrow I'll go over to Carlos' depot and get first hand news of him before I go. Baby, this kind of thing is happening everywhere. But it makes no difference. I don't know how I'll bear being parted from you. When we'll meet again only God knows; I can't tell!" He held her, trembling, filled with tortuous emotion. It was unbelievably difficult for a man to be torn away from his beloved.

"Don't worry too much, darling, We'll be all right together. The baby will be old enough to take notice of you when you come home. Ruth won't leave us, and Carlos, from time to time, will come home. The only one of our little family who'll give cause for anxiety will be Simon. He's so nervous, and depends so much on me. In fact, the arrival of the baby may make him quite jealous. But have no fear, I'll be able to cope. After all, having babies is woman's work!" Lifting his hand and placing the palm across her cheek firmly, he said, "Come inside, dear, the news will shortly be on and I don't like to miss it."

Emma, Ruth and Simon lived quietly together, the two women with their own private worries. Ruth seldom received news of Tom, and after an air raid on London, she patiently waited the next day for a telephone call from him. Sometimes she had to wait several days, but she remained calm, although her nerves were like a razor's edge. She was very fond of Simon, but Carlos was her favourite, with his warm smile, gay whistle and an abundance of good cheer. She listened eagerly to his letters which Emma read aloud and, she knitted for him, made cakes to send to him, and was happy whenever he got weekend leave. Emma's private worry was Carlos and the unborn child. She no longer worried that she was cheating, or fostering someone else's child on to Andrew. Life was now so uncertain - war made one feel lighter in responsibilities - anything could happen any day, any minute. She feared for Carlos' safety; she feared for the little one coming into such a world. Without Ruth she would be alone in the world. Isobel was driving a mobile canteen around bomb areas, George was somewhere with the army abroad. Her mother-in-law was quite wisely in California, and many people she knew were now scattered or already killed. She trembled as she thought of Andrew, gone God knows where, and all she could do was wait and wait. She missed him sorely; letters and cards were so far between, and never gave any indication of where he was. All he could do was to send her his undying love. She was getting near her time, and thought it best to tell Simon that there would be soon a new member in the family.

"What do you mean, mother?" He called her mother now. Carlos has said, "Look, Simon, now that I'm going away, you must be quite grown up, and look after mother. Drop the mummy and dadda. Mother and Father sounds much better. Be kind to mother, try to keep that temper in check when things go wrong - look after my dog, old chap, and when father goes away, be a man around the house!"

Simon, with adoring eyes that quickly swam with tears, had looked up at Carlos and assured him he would do his best, both by mother and the dog Judy. "After all," he'd said, "I am nearly nine, and I'll soon be as tall as you." And stretching up on his toes he'd tried to expand his chest. So when Emma informed him of a new member joining the family, he naturally thought of some adult.

"What do you mean, mother?" he said, "are we going to have someone like Auntie Ruth to live here?"

"No, my darling, someone much more important than that. We're going to have a little baby, a little brother or sister for you and Carlos!"

Rage, jealous rage, surged up within him! How dare mother bring another baby into their home! A baby would take all her attention, he would be left out of things and take second place. He would hate it, he knew he would. He loved his mother: he only wanted his mother. He never minded sharing her with father and Carlos because they loved him back. But this baby didn't know him, wouldn't love him! It would want everyone's attention. Emma was talking; she could see the doubts and jealousies passing across his countenance.

"To have a little baby to look after will be wonderful, my darling. I'll rely on you so much to help me. There's Auntie Ruth to look after our home, and you'll help look after me and the new baby. We'll have heaps of happy days to tell Carlos and father about when they come home."

"Will you love me just the same, mother? Will you hug me and kiss me as you always do?"

She clutched him closely to her and fiercely said, "Always and always, my darling", her tears mingling with his. They comforted each other.

A few days later Ruth went to London. She was more than anxious for Tom. There had been very heavy bombing around the docks, and London had been ablaze for days. The firemen, Home Guard, and ARP worked incessantly to overcome the disaster. Hundreds had lost their lives; there seemed no end to the devilry of the enemy.

"I won't be away longer than three days, Emms, but I must find out about Tom. The local nurse'll come directly you phone for her - yes, I know you have a few more weeks yet, and I know you haven't much faith in her because she's elderly and come out of retirement. But Dr Harvey has great faith in her. My real concern is leaving you alone at nights - shall I find someone to come in? I know how nervous you can get."

Putting on a brave face, and hoping to send Ruth away cheerfully, Emma said, "Now, don't worry, Ruth. I'll be perfectly all right. I'm sure what you say about Sister Manning is true. As to being nervous (please God, I'm not) well, the nights are very short, and daylight soon comes again." With that reassurance, Ruth departed.

That night Emma could not sleep. Simon shared her room, "to look after you while Auntie is away". She trembled with fear as she lay in the gathering night. So many things seemed to haunt her. She thought of the mother she would never know, the only mother she had ever known, and wondered, as she often did, why she had been discarded. She remembered her foster mother, the only mother she had ever known, and the happy days in their poverty when she was first widowed. She thought of Uncle George, and Auntie Maggie, of the boys she used to play with, Willy Martain and Albert Peggs. And then Diane and John, their love, and untimely end. The horror of finding them, the smiling Diane beneath the bower of flowers. Where were they now? What were they doing?

The baby jumped about in her belly with extreme vigour as her imagination saw once again Diane and John, the latter in the pool of blood. She sweated, she trembled, as did the child, and she stifled a scream as a window rattled gently in the early morning breeze. And then she heard his voice, no, not Andrew's - Henry's - it seemed to say, "Be quiet, Emms, All's well, I gave you my heart long ago - I'll always be with you".

"Henry, oh Henry," she called as though he was near, "I'm so frightened." And then another voice consoled her: "Go to sleep, Babe, your old Uncle is looking after you." She was now sobbing quietly to herself. She stuffed her handkerchief into her mouth, so as not to waken Simon, and in a little while slipped into a dreamless sleep.

The next day Emma tried hard to forget the upset of the previous night. She and Simon had their lunch in the garden, and after resting a while she decided to change her frock, go into the village and see the nurse to ask if she would spend the night with her, as she felt none too well. Crossing the hall hurriedly, her foot shot across the rug at the foot of the stairs. At once a terrific pain tore her stomach almost apart. This is it, she thought; I can't go out, I must wait and see. But the afternoon and evening wore on, and but for a little pain rather like cramp in the lower regions of her stomach, nothing more alarming happened. Her face was burning, and her legs felt weak. Much against his will Simon was put to bed in his own room, and Emma rang the nurse when she thought he was asleep. To her enquiry she was told, "Sister Manning has been in another district working all day, and was expected home more than an hour ago; she'll be told about this immediately she arrives home." She got a similar reply about Dr Harvey. He had been at the local hospital assisting in a major operation, and likewise he would be told. So with that information Emma wisely prepared what was needed for the baby's arrival. There was plenty of hot water, the tiny clothes, and her own clean nightdress hung on a horse around the small bedroom fire she had lit. The windows were slightly opened and a gentle breeze stirred the curtains, so she closed them so that no light could filter through. With difficulty she climbed on to the bed and lay, stiff and tense, and in this position the pains crept down and became worse. She gritted her teeth and in a quiet moment got up and paced the silent room, again gritting her teeth against the urge to scream out. She must be quiet, Simon was just across the dimly-lit landing. Surely either the nurse or doctor would soon come! She ventured to the window and looked out through an inch of parted curtain. A moon shone brightly, and the stars twinkled in the clear night sky. They vanished as a great wave of pain engulfed her. She dropped to the ground, the baby seemed to turn within her, the perspiration poured down her face, the room rocked, she vomited, was spent and lay down.

"Oh God! Oh God!" screamed her silent lips, "send someone to me! I can't bear this alone much longer! Oh, anyone - Ruth -

Andrew - Henry - no, not Henry, he's dead! Oh, anyone, please God, anyone!" Panting and shivering she crawled to the bed; she felt the warmth of the fire, and in a spell of pain relief she once again lay on the bed, drawing the eiderdown over her. Thank God, she thought, no pain but, yes, here it came again. But it had changed its course. It was snapping her spine in two, and not content with that, was spreading itself across either side of her hips, down into her groin, and with it she bore herself down - relief and victory, it had gone, and she relaxed. Her brain was now alert, active, she and her baby was working together. "Simon, oh please sleep, my darling, I'll keep quiet!" She mustn't give in, she must try to count the minutes between each pain. The clock was out of sight; she raised her wrist but her eyes were clouded, her watch covered in mist. The agony became unbearable, the pain unbelievable, creeping steadily round her and down. When it ceased, she breathed gently, wiped the sweat from her blinded eyes. No thoughts now for any other being, just for her and the baby. She saw her tight belly, and in curiosity watched the movements. It seemed to strain and fight. Time was forgotten. Shock upon shock, then exhaustion. The baby fought. Emma's hands clenched either side of her, pushing into the mattress, feet apart, pressing with tigerish strength against the bed rail, blood trickling from her bottom lip as her teeth sank into it, straining - straining. A time of unconsciousness - how long? a second? eternity? She dragged back to the inferno, they both fought on together. The vagina stretched, and closed - the baby fought on, Emma more exhausted - straining - straining; her brain was clouding; somewhere faintly she heard a voice - she was pushed on to her side, her legs were lifted apart, one raised, and came to rest upon the nurse's shoulder.

She said, "Nearly ready, doctor, but she's too exhausted - a little chloroform will help!"

Energy returned. Emma turned her head and let out a scream, "No, no, I'll do it alone, leave me, I want to do it alone!"

"Hush, my dear, it's all right!" said the soothing voice of Doctor Harvey, "we'll all help together. Keep her leg on your shoulder, nurse, and you, my dear, push, push. That's right, a little harder - come on, a little more - ah! that's better!" And then there was a terrific rush, the baby's head, the shoulders, and it had entered the world. It yelled in protest. Her leg came to rest against the other and her stomach was pummelled until it was drained and now loose. She closed her eyes, only to open them quickly as the nurse's voice reached her.

"Don't you want to see your baby, Lady Craig? You have another little boy!" She saw the tiniest morsel sitting on one hand of the nurse, supported by the other hand and arm - its little head surrounded by long black hair, the eyelids closed. It was beautiful, exquisite, and as the nurse wrapped a shawl round it Emma softly said, "Hello, my darling. Hello Jonathan!" And so he was named. It was the thirteenth of June.

Later, when Emma awoke from a soothing sleep, Jonathan lay in his cot beside her. The nurse and doctor had gone and miraculously Ruth was hovering near; beside her stood Simon. A rush of protective love enveloped her, she drew Simon down to her, saying softly, "We have another little boy, darling; you have a dear little brother", and he replied, "I know mother, because I saw an angel in the night cross the landing into your room, and then I heard the baby cry, and I knew Jesus had answered my prayers." Later, the nurse said it must have been herself as she came from the bathroom. The footsteps and murmurings, or maybe one of Emma's screams, had awakened Simon. Anyway, it was a beautiful way to think. From then on Simon regarded Jonathan as his very own property, and all the futures of the three brothers were held closely together by a deep love which had originated in the womb of the woman who bore them, and who was long the centre of their lives.

Chapter Fourteen

Two years had passed; Emma remained in the cottage with Ruth and her two young sons. Andrew was in the Middle East, and despite the confidence she had had that the war would end before another two years elapsed, it dragged on. Carlos had, according to Army records, attained the age eighteen, and was now transferred to the militia. Alone, Emma could not stand up to Carlos and insist he tell his correct age; she was alone, lonely, she loved him fiercely, and when he reasoned with her, she felt he was right.

"Don't try to stop me, mother," he had said, "I want to go overseas, I enjoy army life. If you do intervene, I'll only join up again in another name. I don't want to, but I will if I have to. After all, we're all in this war together, whether we wear a uniform or not!"

"But Carlos," interposed Emma, her eyes immediately swimming with tears, "suppose you get killed, suppose you're taken prisoner, what shall I do?"

Laughingly, he put his arm around her and drew her near. "Mother, dear, with you it's suppose, suppose, but it's not good to sit on the edge of a precipice. All we fear never comes true. And even if I were killed," he said this with the flippancy of youth, "I'll know nothing about it."

"But I shall, dear. I'll know, and suffer for it, and because of it, for as long as I live."

"You talk as though I have only one parent. What about father? He has feelings too, and although he'll be very angry to know what I've decided to do, he'll understand. So let's look forward to the time when the war is over and we'll all be together again."

"What optimism!" thought Emma, and retreated. That leave, which was the last before he left England, Carlos spent with his mother and his two brothers. He knew how she was suffering, and did his best to make her happy. He himself was very happy about the future, and looked forward very much to confronting the enemy. He was young, full of life, full of daring. Simon enjoyed his company, and was thrilled that he had such a wonderful, brave brother.

One morning Emma heard Carlos talking to Jonathan. He had the little chap astride his knees.

"Just you be a good little scout while your Carlos is away. When I come home again, you'll be a bigger boy, and will be old enough to go rabbiting with Simmy and me. I'll make you a bow and arrow; we'll take my canoe and sail on the Dart, and the three of us will go camping. What'd you think of that, Sim? We'll have lots of fun."

Simon, now raising ten, looked adoringly at his hero brother and then at Jonathan. "Yes, it'll be fun when you come home again - and we will make toffee and bake buns as we used to? You'll love Carlos' toffee, Jon - we can't make any now because of rationing, but we will!"

Emma looked at her three sons, tall, handsome Carlos, only his height to remind her of Henry; Simon, so like Andrew, fair, slight, strong-willed, and at times a little arrogant; and the baby Jonathan, a replica of Carlos, every feature, poise of the head, sunny smile, sweetest of tempers, lovable, cuddly. How she loved them; she was proud of her first-born, protective of her second, and filled with embracing love for the youngest. Sons, yes, they were what she had wanted - no daughters - just sons. She was satisfied.

So Carlos departed. They stood at the gate as he once again swung down the lane towards the little station. He was whistling, and turned every now and then to wave to them. To say goodbye on a station platform was too distressing. They liked it better this way. Jonathan was in Ruth's arms, Emma with Simon stood very close, for he was bravely trying to hide his tears, and Judy, the dog, pulled on her lead, held firmly by Simon, because she would have gone after her young master. The lane took a bend, and Carlos stopped. He took off his hat and waved quickly, turned and was gone. Simon burst into tears, Jonathan, to keep him company, did likewise, Judy strained on her leash and Ruth clutched it. The two women staggered back along the drive, both blinded by tears, and once inside the hall, Emma went to her room, lay across the bed and cried as though her heart would break. Because of what she had done, because of

Henry, because of so much that was locked in her heart, she knew that for him, for her handsome Carlos, she had a special love.

Cheerful little notes came intermittently from Carlos during the next two weeks. There was an occasional letter from Andrew and then for the next harrowing month, silence. Emma scanned the press, listened to the radio news, hoping she might discover some news of her beloved ones. She did; Andrew was a prisoner of war in the Far East, Carlos was in Palestine. He wrote:

"Dearest Mother,

I'm very well, extremely fit, nevertheless I feel great concern for you since receiving your letter telling me of father's captivity We here are in great spirit, and have every confidence that the war will be won by the Allied Forces, and very soon too. It's certainly very frustrating for father to be taken prisoner. I hope the near future will bring his quick release. In the meantime, have a brave heart, and a stiff upper lip. Give my love to Simon and Jonathan. I have a number of souvenirs for them. Much love,

Carlos.

PS Sorry, I forgot Auntie Ruth. My love to her, and I hope she'll soon be better."

And so Emma's anxious mind worked on. She drew the children closer to her, was more protective, fierce almost in her love for them; and meanwhile, she watched Ruth, who silently went about the house, looking terribly ill and often crying. Tom was up north working in another shipyard - the London docks had been sadly crippled - and she longed so much to be with him. But it was impossible to join him, and they both had to be content with their frequent letters - which really did not tell either very much. She did not know that he was living in poor surroundings, missing his home and her, working twelve hours a day on merchant ships that were badly damaged by the enemy. He just tried to be as cheerful as he could, and wrote light-hearted letters. He did not know that she had seen a specialist and that her sickness was incurable, not until it was too late - too late, almost, to say goodbye.

One night Ruth was taken so very ill that within a few hours she had been whisked away to hospital and operated on. It was just a temporary relief. Emma had to face the fact that Ruth would soon die. The tumour was malignant. Daily she travelled to the hospital; Tom came to stay with her, and when the parting came, it was very quiet and peaceful.

"Don't cry, Emms," Ruth whispered, "I'm not in any more pain, and I'm content."

Emma left the little ward, blinded by unshed tears. A few days later they buried Ruth, Tom returned north, and she saw him no more.

Memories are precious things, and memories of Ruth remained for ever throughout Emma's life. When she was older Emma always recalled clearly that part of her life she had shared with Ruth.

It was November 1943 and the winter, lonely and bleak, was well upon them. The fears of her youth began to creep upon her at night, until in the end she put up a camp bed in the boys' room for company. They asked no questions. Simon continued his day school, Jonathan grew closer than ever to her. A daily woman helped to run the house, and Emma tried to busy herself in the garden and clear away the autumn foliage. But it all seemed so dead, dead as Ruth, dead as Henry, dead as any of the bright spirits that had once lived happily in the animated Emma.

There was no news of Andrew, letters from Carlos became less and less frequent - when they arrived they were brief, gave no news of himself, and it was evident that correspondence was heavily censored. Very little news came from her mother-in-law in America, and when it did it was fretful and complaining. Emma's mother, lived in Suffolk and seemed to take life philosophically. Her life's motto, What's to be, will be was still accepted. She wrote seldom, and when she did seemed to have little to say. Emma, despite the fact that she had a reliable income, seemed hemmed in. The boys took up quite a lot of her time, and when they were at school there seemed little to do. She hated knitting, even for the Forces; she no longer wanted to help with the Red Cross. She wrote innumerable letters to Andrew, hoping that one day the Red Cross would see he received them. She wrote to Carlos, Isobel, George; she entertained members of the Forces who were stationed nearby. But all the time she suffered a lack of fulfilment. Her body needed sexual satisfaction - she wondered how other women were enduring long separations, and fully understood why many of them committed adultery. It was difficult. She was surprised that her mind, when she travelled alone over the past, more often lingered on Henry's love-making, and much more vividly than upon Andrew's. She told herself that she loved Andrew very, very much, and yet it was Henry she mostly thought of. Not Andrew - Henry, whose memory was still so vivid. It was Henry's voice that she heard, Henry's arms that she felt about her, and even the smell of his skin seemed to once again assail her nostrils. She felt ashamed and angry with herself that he should come so readily to her, and remorseful that he should have, even in dreams, priority over Andrew. She would tell herself it was really because she had cheated Henry of his son, or was it sons? She would never know - but now that he was dead his memory could awaken so much. But she doubted. Had he not said to her: "I will leave my heart with you - roses I would shower on you - red roses for love"? Was it not possible that one could love two people at the same time? Oh, she was a complex person! She was a romantic; she must put aside these thoughts, these imaginings, and keep only Andrew and her sons in her mind and heart. But she never did. In all the years that followed, Henry never released her. A quick glance at Carlos' photograph, a gentle hand that seemed to touch her heart, a warm summer breeze, and a vase of crimson roses could all remind her that quietly, silently, and almost triumphantly Henry had taken possession, had remained to be with her forever. Sometimes she felt grateful, especially during the nights of her terror. He was so close that he comforted her. In the daytime, her guilt was upon her, and so to recompense the unsuspecting Andrew, she drew Simon closer to her. She loved dear, darling, independent Jonathan, but Simon she almost devoured. She began to see in him something spiritual. She concentrated on his religious life, she encouraged him in every possible way to be devout. Simon at that age was very intense.

The local vicar was also the tutor for religious instruction at Simon's school, so it was easy for Emma to see that he encouraged Simon to attend church regularly; to entertain the vicar in her home, for she had made up her mind that Simon should be a priest. Of her three children, she told herself, he was the one she had planned to have - he was the one who, from the beginning, was welcomed into this world. She had been so very wicked, had failed always to make amends. Simon would be the one who would eventually intercede between herself and her Maker. Silly, stupid Emma! But after this confirmation, it was Simon who definitely made up his mind.

"Mother," he said, "the Head told us in hall last week that those of us who had seriously given thought to confirmation should leave their names with the vicar when he came next. I've seriously made up my mind, and given my name. Are you confirmed, mother?"

"No, my darling, I'm not. I should be, I suppose, but up to now I've given no thought to it. Carlos should have been confirmed - I'm very neglectful." She gave a watery smile, expecting Simon to find an excuse for her, but was disappointed that he made no comment. His religious teachings were now taken seriously, and the vicar often came to the cottage, showing a great deal of interest in Simon. Very often he went to the vicarage for tennis and became a great favourite with the vicar's wife. Simon had a charm that drew people to him. He was serious, and yet he could at times be most humorous. He was a trifle arrogant, but this Emma excused, for she knew he had inherited much of his character and disposition from Andrew and his family. He liked things to be right, he was exacting in all he undertook. Unlike his elder and younger brothers, he was extremely tidy, and would know immediately when entering his bedroom if any of his books had been lifted from the shelves and replaced again. Emma was very proud of all this. She thought it was wonderful to have produced a son like Simon. He worked hard at school, had a deep regard for his father's family, was exceedingly proud of both father and Carlos, and adored Jonathan. To his mother he gave the deepest love that a son can give. He adored her, thought her charming, witty, gay and beautiful. When alone, he sought her company. Sometimes he would show his temper over trivial things, and this would hurt her exceedingly. Quietly he would go away to his room and pray for forgiveness, and pay penance by refusing those little delicacies that Emma tried to get for her sons during that awful time of rationing. Then the ready smile would leave her countenance, she would find solace in little Jonathan; remorse would fill Simon for the hurt he had inflicted, and he would plead forgiveness, which was readily given. The sun would come out again on their little world.

"The trouble with me, mother," she remembered he had said on one occasion, "The trouble is, I love you so much that when I get into a temper it's you I want to hurt the most. I love you so very, very much!"

"Do you, dear?" she asked with great satisfaction, all hurt having disappeared. "Do you, my darling? I hope you always will."

And so the lives of all three were bound so closely together in that little cottage - waiting for Carlos' letters, waiting for news of Andrew - time ticked away until May 15th, VE day.

Chapter Fifteen

The whole country, it seemed to Emma, rose in one loud cheer of victory! Bonfires were lit on the hilltops, in the lowlands, on street corners. Celebrations burst out everywhere. Yet Emma could not raise one spark of enthusiasm. Somehow the haste to celebrate was almost indecent. Hospitals everywhere were full of the injured and dying. True, there would be no more air raids, rockets would cease ravaging the unsuspecting, the enemy was vanquished, the allies victorious. But the greater the jubilations, the louder the cheering, the more heavily gloom settled upon Emma. She should be happy now, she told herself. Andrew would be coming home, Carlos too, and then they would all be together again. She tried to plan, but the little flame of enthusiasm flickered out before long. She took down the blackout and was thankful for that.

The days passed and June brought beautiful weather. And still she waited. Jonathan was a happy little boy and did not notice her quiet demeanor, but Simon, the sensitive one, was soon aware of it, and without speaking of this inner sadness in his mother, he drew very close to her. In his childish way he wanted to protect her, and at every turn he was at hand. She waited - for what? She could not tell - letters from Andrew and Carlos? Yes, that was it, yes, that was the reason for her despondency; she was alone, with only the two children. Ruth was gone, so was Henry, who had adored her; Andrew was suffering God knows what, and Carlos, her darling boy, her brave one - what had become of him? She had been too long in the cottage, nearly four years; it would be better when they were home together. Of course, she was stale, she had done so very little. The beautiful summer that lay before them would coax her back to her bright self. She must be cheerful, she must sing as she used to, not only for her own sake, but for the children. Simon's anxious concern must be allayed.

She went into the garden, determined to be energetic, and Judy's bark of welcome told her the post mistress was about to come up the drive. She walked towards her with a welcoming smile, but before the smile could leave her lips and lighten her eyes, it suddenly froze; for now she knew, she knew the reason for her gloom, for the days filled with despair and lethargy. It was here, before her, in the proffering hand of the post mistress, a telegram, a small piece of paper, as shattering as any torpedo that had ever been fired, fatal, final, tottering her world! She knew - it was Carlos! With trembling fingers she took it, not glancing at the grave face before her. Tears were already blinding her. She tottered towards the house, sat down in the porch and, with unseeing eyes, lowered her head, and remained motionless.

And so she learned how he had died of poliomyelitis. And with later correspondence she was told how he had been stricken on May 27, in Piagimea, a town in Northern Italy, and had been flown down to Florence, put on an iron lung, and three days later had died. On June 2nd, his dear body had been given its last resting place, and the number of his grave was sent by his Commanding Officer, with his deepest sympathy.

The days of agony, deep, deep agony began. Emma's every nerve, every sense screamed out for the bitter injustice of it all. Oh, to die herself! "Oh, my darling son, so tall and handsome. For me to suffer is all I ask, for ever and ever, if only your God could have made a mistake, and it wasn't Carlos who had died. Punish me, God, for the wickedness that is in me, but please, oh, please send him home." In the darkness of her room at night, when the children slept, she knelt praying, confessing openly:

"I have always been wilful, lustful and a cheat. I twisted the heart of Henry, and denied him his son; I deceived Andrew, and continued to do so all our married life; I was openly prepared to cheat darling Simon of his birthright. Ruth, I used for my own selfish ends, I forsook my stepmother who, in her own way, tried to rear me. My natural mother I have cursed - oh God, oh God - punish me, make me eat the dust, but send Carlos home to me. I will make amends."

And then, when she was calmer and hysteria departed, her prayers were more contrite. "Dear God, for Thy Son's sake, hear my prayer. I pray for my beloved son, Carlos. I accept thy will. I know that millions of other mothers are suffering as I am suffering. Hear their prayers and comfort them. Give Carlos the continuous assurance of your love. Gather him, dear Jesus, in the loving fold of your arms. Forgive him any little trespasses, for little I know they were. He was so young, dear Lord. If he is bewildered, help him. I thank you for the beauty of him. I am so truly sorry for my sins, and through this agony that I am called upon to endure, I hope to be a better person and love Thee more. Thank you for Andrew, for my younger sons, for those that have loved me, and now departed this life. Look down upon me, dear Lord, hear my prayers, and comfort me. Amen."

The days went by, short or long, she did not know. There was Simon to comfort, Jonathan to play with, and a daily diary to keep for Andrew. But the agony dragged on, and sometimes it seemed almost impossible to endure. It would be best to think of Carlos alive, as though any day he would be home. She would play a game to suit the unhappy Simon too. So they began to talk of Carlos, and remember together so much about him. It brought, at first, a watery smile to Simon's face; then, youth having a happy disposition, Simon would join in the laughter at some of Carlos' past pranks. Jonathan was never involved, for Carlos was mostly just a name to him. Emma suffered, suffered more than she could ever imagine a human being could, but as time passed she began to accept it, and so it became easier.

It might have eased the pain, though she could never have shared it, if Andrew had been home, or been somewhere where she could write to him, and he to her; for over the past two years she had had no news of him, so he too could be dead. If not, how was he? she asked herself. Could the strength of his love remain, what had captivity done to him? How much had he suffered, both physically and spiritually? He must now know that they were no longer at war. How long would the wheels of officialdom take to turn before he was released? And when released, how would he be? How would they both be? Everything had died within her. Fiercely, too fiercely she loved her two remaining boys. A yearning to almost absorb Simon overcame her. He, and not Jonathan, was the only living creature beside herself who had known so intimately, so closely, her beloved Carlos. There was a bond between them that Emma in her agony was tightening daily. Simon, the uncertain, the loving, the clinging and often demanding true son of her marriage was like a piece of flotsam in the swift flowing stream of life, and like a weak swimmer she had grasped at it, and was relieved that eventually she would get to the land safely. Of his future she did not think, and how he would break the bonds of her absorbing love was left to the future. But here they were now, loving each other, loving Jonathan, talking of Carlos and waiting for Andrew.

Two years later, in the autumn, he came. Emma opened the London house. It was dirty, tired and fusty. She waited. The boys were now both at Westminster school. With heart racing, eyes searching, she went to Victoria Station. The milling crowds of people, all waiting as she was waiting, frightened her. Train after train came in, unloading their human cargoes. Voices were raised, screams of children rose, restless; they wanted to run with each other and play. But their mothers clung to their hands, hoping to show off the offspring of that last union. Emma sat on a seat quite close to one of the arrival platforms. She had sat there for three hours. The elated feeling she had had when the first train arrived had quietly disappeared as each one brought disappointment. Fear began to take possession of her. He was ill - too ill to travel - he had arrived, she had missed him, he had gone home! No, of course he had not gone home, he had not come, he could not come! She was alone, just with the boys - Andrew was dead! He could have been dead a long time. This should not be a new grief, she should have grieved when he had died. It was cruel that he should have died, perhaps more than a year ago, and only now she was to grieve! Everyone who had loved her had gone. Full of pity for herself, she thought of Henry. How sad it was that he had gone, but so very convenient for her future life with Andrew. But there was no future with him. He, too, had loved her and was gone. And so was Carlos, who had always adored her. All she had ever wanted from life was to be loved; was that asking too much?

Small she was, and as she sat crouched in the railway seat she looked shrivelled and obscure. Tears of pity welled into her eyes; she thought now only of Andrew - the day they had first met in the Louvre; the evening at Montmarte, Florence, Venice, and how happy they had always been together. His acceptance of Carlos, his ignorance of Henry, oh, so much! And now she was without him! During his captivity she had always hoped (she was by nature an optimist), but now hope had disappeared. She dried her eyes and began to rise from her seat. The final few of a trainload of soldiers were leaving the barrier. She must go home; there was no need to wait longer. She glanced towards the last soldier as he came through; they looked at each other for a second that was eternity, a pair of hands clutched her, a trembling voice, or was it two that spoke at the same time? Emma! Andrew! It was unbelievably true - he was here - he was alive, it was a resurrection! They did not utter another word, and it wasn't until they settled into a taxi that she heard his voice properly again, and then she knew her Andrew, her husband, her beloved had returned!

From then on, the going was hard. They found they were almost strangers. He could not adjust himself easily. The children, though delighted to have him home, continued to direct their lives towards their mother. It was only natural she supposed, and she did nothing to alter it.

Unfamiliar with the nature of Andrew's life as a prisoner, she felt bewildered that his excitement at resuming his sex life with her was very remote. He had tried to please her, but up till now he could not function. She told him she understood, and was patient. Nevertheless it did not satisfy the craving needs of her starved body. At first, she thought sleeping separately would help solve the problem, but then she did not suggest it for fear of hurting him. Andrew spoke little of his captivity, and after a while she ceased to ask him questions because she saw how withdrawn he became when it was mentioned. He went out little, and having seen so much death, the loss of Carlos caused him pain, but no shock or surprise. He did his best to understand what the loss meant to Emma, but she realised that he was aware that he failed miserably. His health had suffered very much; he had been a constant victim of dysentry and beri beri. She saw a terrific scar across his stomach and asked if he had been wounded. With a sickly, crooked smile he had said, "No. not wounded in the way you're thinking. This scar is the result of a mere removal of my appendix. The Nippon had a diabolical way of removing it. It took a week of carving before the thing was eventually removed!" Then, seeing the horror on her face, he tried to soften the information he was giving her. "You see," he continued, "according to them, as an officer, I was always interfering with their administration towards the men around me. On one occasion I actually snatched a strap from a thug who was beating a dying man who had collapsed at his gruelling job of hacking a tree. Oh, I could tell you a lot more! So when I went down with this appendix, since I was unpopular, and with our medical men working themselves to death without the medical aid that was necessary to them, one of their butchers gleefully stepped in, and experimented without any anaesthetic. Oh, hell, why must I talk about it? forget it!"

She didn't talk about it any more; she didn't forget it either, but left it very wisely to the future. Time passed, they saw few people. Andrew, still uncertain, was receiving medical aid; but he did not reveal that, try as he might, he could not be a husband to Emma. He would watch Emma through half-closed eyes as he lay in bed, removing her clothes, brushing her hair, the gentle rhythm of her arms as she stroked her hair, and that uplifting of her breasts, and her body would sway with the rhythm, but his mind that tried to imagine her body close to him, beneath him, enjoying again the possession of each other, could not transmit the desired effect, and he would pretend, when she eventually got into bed and felt the sweet nearness of her body, that he was asleep. And so time went on, and their thoughts and hunger each for each other continued.

After a period of rehabilitation Andrew took up the reigns of his old business. It was indeed hard going; it was almost extinct, and it would take years to rebuild. It seemed that hardly anyone drank in England; no one could afford to, either, on the war-scarred continent, and so Andrew turned his attention to America, and endeavoured to trade a little there. It was hard going. His mother remained in California, and he decided to join pleasure with business and visit her. The boys, he told Emma, would be quite all right. They were now boarders at school, and so they could spend two months on their travels.

"First of all, Emma, we shall go to Florence, and visit Carlos' grave; from there to Paris, and then to America." But she would not agree to go without him in that order.

"How can we go back to these places yet?" she said sadly. "Paris is now filled with so much sadness, Andrew; the horror of Diane's death, but it would soon come back again in a city that must be filled with the horrors of recent years. I know we met there, but it's far too early to recapture anything we ever found there. In Florence it would be the same. The beautiful days at the Villa are overshadowed with my darling's grave - I could find no joy in going with you - and when I do, for the first time, I must go alone. Darling, let us go straight to America; I shall like that best."

Not feeling up to arguments of any description, Andrew agreed. They set sail for New York. The crossing was very agreeable, they enjoyed it even though the cuisine was sparse. Emma, romantic as ever, felt how wonderful it would be if only Andrew desired her physically. It could be a honeymoon! Sometimes she found him watching her, and sometimes she was hopeful, but he would continue to ignore, or perhaps not see her intimate self - not since this one attempt to love her had he ever approached her since. She felt at times old, unwanted. Never did she hear him call her Baby; never did he kiss her as in the old days. Kiss her he did, but only gently on either cheek, seldom on the lips. She had tried many seductive ways to encourage him, but had given up in vain. And now here they were in New York, booking into the Waldorf, being shown into a beautiful suite, almost bridal. They dressed for dinner and, almost as in a dream danced together, as they had in that far distant Florence. They walked together arm in arm, as they had always done, oh, so very long ago, and then back to their suite. A few drinks were sent up, but Emma could not take any. Tears were not far away; it was all such a mockery. She prepared for bed, while Andrew went into the dressing-room. She plaited her hair, turned off the lights except the small glow over the bed, and got in. She closed her eyes and did not see

Andrew's pyjamaed figure enter. Suddenly the room was in darkness, Andrew beside her. He swooped over her, stifling her protests with his mouth; she managed to utter a few incoherent words, then forcing his knee between her legs he possessed her. The tremors and rapture that she had known so well in the past left her breathing quickly. His inflamed passion of sheer lust brought a burst of equal passion from her. It seemed his thrusts were those of anger, gaining victory after victory. until with a quiver he sagged and fell beside her, pressed his face into her bare shoulder, took her breast between his hands, kissed its hard nipple. She clung to him; they lay together a long while, almost welded together, and then suddenly he began to sob as though his heart would break. She stroked his brow, saying nothing, and finally they went to sleep. Emma did not refer to it next morning - she gladly accepted the knowledge that Andrew wanted and needed her. She knew how unhappy he had been, and that to accept this was best for them both. She loved him and he began to tell her the same. He again called her baby, he seemed to be aware of his virility and, whenever he wanted her, she was ready to receive him. No thought of whether she would conceive entered her head. He was her own dear Andrew again - all was well. Strangely enough Emma was never with child again, but Andrew, in all their future together, did not mention this to her, nor she to him. After a week of being so close together, love-making whenever they wanted, Andrew said a startling thing.

"Emma, we'll be happy together, I know. Since I've been home from prison camp I've fought hard not to love you as I did in the past. I could never suffer, I thought, as I did from those years of separation from you. Gradually, you began to fade. I did everything I could to wipe you from my memory, from my heart. In its place I received the knowledge of your infidelities both before and after we were married - oh yes, I knew all about them, but I loved you and said nothing. Then, I would tell myself, if I don't come out of this, Carlos, whom I loved, but not so well as Simon, my own son, would take from my son his inheritance. I began to hate you as much as I had loved you. But other memories would rush in, and so my hatred was not complete. I purposely boarded the last train that day to

Victoria, in order to delay our meeting. And when we did meet, I couldn't resume my life with you. I sometimes felt desire as I watched you, but it passed in a flash, and yet contact with you reopened all the old loving and desires. The charm you held for me when we first met is upon me once again. Your love for me has awakened mine for you. I find I'm yours as much as I ever had been. I find comfort in you, I love everything about you. If there was anything to forgive, it's over now. The brave front you put up at the loss of Carlos, whom I know was your beloved child, makes me humble in your presence. I can only guess, I shall never know your suffering, and since I came home, I have added greatly to it. Forgive me, my darling, I'll do my best to make you happy."

Wisely, Emma put her arms around him. He held her close, her eyes brilliant with unshed tears. "Forgive me, to, my darling," she murmured, and silently whispered, "Forgive me, too, Henry and Carlos, and may Jonathan never know."

After two months in America, visiting Andrew's mother and such old friends as the Ferraris, they made their way home. Bravely Emma agreed to spend a few days in Paris. She visited John's grave; Diane's body had been taken to England for burial. She lingered for a while beside the tombstone. It was neglected, overgrown. She placed some flowers on his grave, and waited for a while, thinking of Diane and John, the love they must have had for each other, the final action which ended it all. She no longer feared what she had seen, it was now so long ago. She, too, had been wayward, but Fate had treated her more kindly - or had it? The open wound reminded her of the small but very heavy cross she must silently carry to the end of her days.

Andrew was in conference with some business acquaintances, so from the English cemetery she walked as she had done when a girl, new in Paris, thrilled with the city and adventure. Along the Seine she passed the Palais de Justice, its walls blackened with age, towards the Notre Dame, beautiful in the golden afternoon sunshine, over the Ponte Marie, and then to the Ile de Saint Louis. The shadow of the old Emma followed. She sat awhile on a low parapet and gazed at the river. Suddenly she felt unburdened, free. She rose, recrossed the bridge, turned and gazed upon the overhanging foliage of the trees as they bent in almost farewell, farewell to her, as she left, the old Emma, the little Cockney kid, in the eerie shadows of the falling sun.

They then went to Florence. It was very depressing, its people poor and in the aftermath of war, the villa where they had lived stood empty and neglected. Emma did not wish to stay, only to visit Carlos' grave. The War Graves Commission was trying to do its best to lay lawns and make paths between the rows of graves. They found his grave, the end of a row. It was trim and well cared for. A wooden cross marked his resting place, with the River Arno gently passing nearby. Andrew left Emma as she knelt down. Her eyes were dry, her hand steady as she touched the cross, her lips mobile. She pictured him, her tall, dark handsome Carlos, just a foot or so away, wrapped in a blanket, those beautiful eyes closed for ever. "Would he know now?" she thought. "Has he forgiven me if he does know? Everything is so hard to understand, my darling. Henry, your father, forgave me a long time ago. Love is a very confusing thing at times, but this I know, my darling: I loved you, I love you, and in my heart, selfish as it may be, your memory will be evergreen."

Andrew was beside her and helped her to rise. He gently kissed her. "Goodbye, old chap," he murmured, and to Emma he said, "Have you noticed how each grave has two bushes? Here on Carlos' there's a rosemary bush and a rose bush. When the buds open, I feel sure they'll be red."

As they walked away she heard a voice on the breeze, so very quiet, only for her: "Red roses for love, my darling!" and then it faded with a sigh. A smile hovered about her lips, and as she reached the gate and looked back, "And Rosemary for remembrance!" she replied.